Home Group

Home Group

Jim White

DEDICATED TO MA, JUDIE, MIKE T., AND LISA

SPECIAL THANKS TO

COOPER HOSPITAL'S TRAUMA/ICU Department for treating Jimmy with the care and dignity that all people deserve in the hours before their passing. As a member of Jim's family, I want you to know that your kindness to us, on March 27, 2004, will not be forgotten.

Sincerely,
Holly Donahue, Jim's Sister

Chapter One

"Well, what did they say, Tom?" Dwayne asked.

"Not much," Tom answered.

Tom White and Dwayne sat in the cruiser. Dwayne could tell that Tom was in his usual Sunday morning mood.

Dwayne Cherry was a good cop, maybe too good a cop, to be paired up with the Lieutenant. It was only a temporary set up. Tom's regular partner, Joe "Sugar" Carter, was still in the hospital recovering from a knife wound. Dwayne wasn't very happy about this set up. Every cop in Camden thought he knew how Tom worked. Each had his own idea, but most of them were dead wrong.

Dwayne was about a month away from a soft position in the District Attorney's office. He had wanted this job for the last six months. In his gut he realized that a month with Tom on this detail could ruin his chances.

Dwayne said, "Okay Tom, if you don't want to talk, let's get some grub."

Tom called in and said he'd be out of the car for about thirty minutes. Tom always went to the White Lantern Diner. Dwayne hated the place, but he wasn't about to try to change Tom's habits. He'd go and try to eat something; even though he knew when they threw the food out back, the rats usually turned their noses up at it. He didn't know how the hell Tom survived eating there. Man! It was going to be a long month.

They were passing the High Speed Line parking lot, one of the only useful things built in Camden in the last thirty years, besides the new prison by the Delaware River. It struck Dwayne as odd that the prison, which had the best view of the Delaware and the Philadelphia skyline in all of South Jersey, had no windows in the prison that let you see anything worthwhile. What a waste, he thought.

Dwayne's thoughts of the wasted view came to a sudden stop when Tom said, "About a month."

"What?" Dwayne said.

"They said he'd be out in about a month."

"Oh, that's too bad, I mean that's good, oh shit, I don't know what I mean," Dwayne grumbled. Tom had a really annoying habit of answering a question anywhere from fifteen minutes to two weeks after it was asked, and always looked at you like you were stupid if you didn't realize what he was saying.

They were now driving past the Teamster's Hall, headed for Collingswood Circle, one of Jersey's last remaining traffic circles. The circle is a mess. Sunday morning the traffic is light. By five o'clock on a weeknight, it could take you a half-hour to go the quarter mile around it. At six PM you might get killed just standing near it. Jersey had a lot of circles at one time, but they eliminated most of them, after burying a lot of good people. The problem is that Camden is in South Jersey and the state capital is tuned into North Jersey. There will be a long wait until anything is done about it, if ever.

Once around the circle, it's a short drive to the White Lantern. Tom parked the cruiser out back, between assorted squad cars and K-9 units. Sunday mornings there isn't much going on and most of the guys just drink coffee and grab ass at the Lantern, most of the white guys, that is.

The black cops eat across the street at Joyce's Donuts. That lot's also full of cruisers. Seems like everybody is earning some soft pay this morning. But what the hell, come five o'clock tonight, they'd earn it.

Tom got out of the car and walked across the parking lot to the Lantern. Dwayne followed Tom; half hoping that Willis Taylor wasn't across the street at Joyce's. If Willis saw Dwayne going into the Lantern, he wouldn't miss the opportunity to make something of it.

Willis hated white people and everybody knew it. He was proud of it. He was famous at the station for saying that the goddamn city's eighty percent black, the police force should be eighty percent black. Willis was a good cop, though. He treated all the perps the same . . . like shit . . . famous for never giving anybody a break. Hell, he kicked down his nephew's door when he found out that he was dealing coke. He asked the judge in court to give him the maximum sentence. Told the judge he had personally preached to his nephew since he was six years old, about the risks and the penalties of dealing.

This wasn't so strange. Willis knew most dealers in Camden had a real short life expectancy. Willis drives down to the prison once a week, taking forty dollars to the kid. He makes sure that the kid's wife and child don't want for anything. Go figure! They say that when the kid gets out, he's going to repair computers. Hell, he'll probably earn more than Willis.

Walking into the White Lantern, Tom stepped over a chained and muzzled K-9. It didn't move a muscle.

Following Tom, Dwayne lifted his leg to step over it and the dog was up so fast that he tripped Dwayne, who stumbled into the restaurant, grabbing the counter to stop himself from falling.

Laughter commenced immediately, as Dwayne pulled himself together and straightened his tie.

Ready was down the counter. "Yo, Dwayne, ain't you on the wrong side of the street? The dog ain't used to seeing you over here." More laughter.

With a little anger in his voice, Dwayne says, "Who's the dumb son of a bitch that tied that dog up there?"

Tom put his hand on Dwayne's shoulder. "You okay?" he asked. "Ready, go move the dog."

Ready says, "Don't worry Tom, he only jumps at the brothers, and I don't see any lining up to get in here."

The whole place got quiet. All the cops knew that Ready had just made a mistake. When Tom White told a cop to do something, they knew he meant, now!

Dwayne went to the bathroom to wash up, giving Ready a look that could freeze water on a hot summer day.

From behind the counter, Alice asked Tom, "Two coffees?"

Tom nodded and smiled. Dwayne walked out of the bathroom and took a seat.

Paul Clark and Pete Murphy walked over to Tom and Dwayne.

"Hey Dwayne, how's that good looking wife of yours?"

"Hey Paul, Pete, how you doing? The wife, she's fine. You know her, everything's always fine. She would like to know when you're going to finish the paneling. It's been two weeks."

"I'll be over Saturday morning, bright and early, I swear!" Paul chuckles. "I would have come yesterday, like I said, but the kids are down with something. Hell, it's always something. Look, we gotta get moving. Tom, how's Sug?"

"Sug's gonna be okay," Tom says, "thanks for asking."

"Let's go Pete, and try not to talk too much today," Paul says.

"Goodbye, gentlemen," Pete Clark says.

Everyone put down their coffee to watch Paul and Pete leave.

Frank Jugan says, "Was that Pete Clark? I thought he said 'goodbye, gentlemen'."

Tom says, "Yeah, that was him, he's turning into a real chatter box. Just two days ago, he said, 'Hi, Lieutenant'."

Fred says, "I knew him two years before I was sure he could talk at all. I thought for a while the Mayor was putting a new program forward . . . mute officers."

Tom says, "Listening to you ladies, I think it's a sound idea. Okay guys, I cruised past here on the way to Lourdes, you were all here then, so let's move it."

"Sure Tom, we were just leaving when you and Dwayne pulled up, but we didn't want to seem rude to you and your new partner," Ready says.

As the officers started to file out, Tom called Ready over.

"Ready," Tom said, "what's your detail today?"

"I got the Speed Line," Ready smiles.

"You had the Speed Line. It's Sunday, there's not much there. I've got Gormley on circle traffic but he can cruise the Speed Line every half hour. I want you on Kaighn Avenue, down past West Jersey Hospital. You just park by that Chicken Shack."

"Oh shit, Lieutenant, you serious?" says Ready.

Lieutenant White just stares at him. "When I tell you to move the dog, you move the dog. Now get going."

Alice throws a towel. "Yo, Ready, cry in this."

Dwayne tries not to laugh. Tom's face is deadpan, as usual.

"Fuck you Alice, and have a nice day," Ready says as he leaves.

Tom says to Alice, "If Dwayne would leave, we could go into the kitchen and you could warm something up for me."

"It's always warm for you, good looking." Alice bends down and kisses Tom on the cheek.

Dwayne says, "I don't want to stand in the way of true love, I'll sit in the car."

Alice smiles, "That's not necessary honey, Tom and I have been having this conversation for twenty years and nothing's happened yet. What will it be, boys?"

"I'll take my regular, and top off my coffee. Dwayne, what's for you?"

"I'd like half a grapefruit and a bowl of oatmeal, take the coffee and give me a large Sprite."

"We don't get many orders like that in here. Health kick, huh?" Alice says.

"Always," says Dwayne.

"Honey, you look healthy enough, how about we go in the kitchen and I'll warm something up for you?"

Tom laughs, "Stop it, Alice, I think he's blushing."

"Yeah, I think he is. That's so cute. I'll be right back with your order."

Tom yells through the grimy kitchen doors, "Sweetheart, is that scanner on? I haven't heard a damn thing from it since we came in."

"It's on. It's Sunday morning . . . wait a while," Alice yells over the kitchen noise.

"Dwayne, don't pay any attention to him. He's an idiot, his family tree looks like a flagpole."

"Who? Ready?"

"Yeah, Ready."

"By the way, how's my favorite DA?" Tom asks.

"You heard, huh? DeFrank's okay. Look, I got a chance to move up. I thought I'd take it."

"Sometimes it pays to move a little slower, Dwayne."

"Look, I know a lot of guys think I'm a brown-noser, but the DA's office is a good spot. My wife and I were talking and the way the streets are, lately, it might be the best move. Hell, look what happened to Sugar."

"What happened to Sugar didn't have to happen. He's too big hearted. He's always been that way. The hooker he picked up was whacked. She probably nodded off, came to, realized she was in a cop car and freaked out. She stabs him, friggin' St. Joe 'Sugar' Carter, every hooker's friend."

"Lieutenant White," Dwayne drawls, "are you telling me he picks up hookers, regularly?"

"Listen Dwayne, I love Sugar like a brother, but he makes some bad decisions. Never on a big job . . . he's the best . . . but he loses his perspective with the ladies. Let's face it; if you looked like Sugar, you'd pretty much have to go the hooker route. That's off the record."

"Eggs over easy, double order of scrapple, grapefruit juice and heavy cream on the coffee. Enjoy."

Dwayne looked at Tom's plate. Alice looked at Dwayne.

"Don't say anything. Let him eat it. He knows it's killing him, but let him eat it."

"I wasn't going to say anything!"

"Good," Tom says as he shovels in his first bite of scrapple.

"Hey! There's something coming over the scanner now," chirps Alice. She loved to hear the police calls. "Holy hell, it's a homicide! They're calling for you," she smiles.

"Why are you so happy?" Tom asks as he pushes his plate away.

"Ah, come on Tom, you know a good murder is great for business. By four this afternoon, every busy body and bored ex-cop, along with every off duty cop, will be in here to talk about it. I've noticed that murder stimulates the appetite. Go get the bad guys, men!" Alice smiles.

"What do I owe you, Alice?" Dwayne asks.

"Nothing, handsome, you're good luck and good for business."

"Alice, you're a ghoul," says Tom.

Alice watched Tom as he drove off in the cruiser with Dwayne. She thought how much she owed him and how he had helped her, so long ago. She was in trouble once, pretty big trouble. Tom took a chance on her, stood up for her in court. Tom told the judge how her family was really her only problem. Her whole family was either in jail or the prison system. Tom suggested to the judge that keeping her locked up for any length of time, would only increase their influence on her. Tom recommended that the judge let her out to work at the White Lantern. He told the judge that cops were there 24 hours a day and when she wasn't working, she could stay at his house for the first year.

It was a weird set up, but Tom always came up that way. For Tom, weird worked. She guessed that was what had made him such a good cop. She was young and pretty with a real smart mouth back then. But Tom's mother won her over with kindness, something so foreign to her that it was uncomfortable.

She remembered her first week at Tom's after getting out on probation. Back then, you could scream at her, slap her, punch her or cut her and she wouldn't even blink. But Tom's mom, her name was Judie, was so nice to her, she'd just go to pieces.

Alice stayed with Judie for five years after Tom moved out. When his mom got the cancer, Alice nursed her eight hours a day after her shift at the Lantern. She wouldn't let a night nurse come in. It was Tom's sister Carol in the day, and Alice at night. Judie and Alice loved each other like mother and daughter.

When Judie died, she left the house to Alice. Nobody else needed it. Tom and Carol were pretty well off. Still, when the Will was read, Alice went to pieces; had a nervous breakdown and was in Our Lady of Lourdes Hospital for two months. Tom asked the shrink to explain her problem to him. He told Tom that when someone was raised like Alice had been, an act of kindness could be stranger and more painful than one can imagine.

When Alice left the hospital, she went back to work at the Lantern. Her house was paid for, so she only had to worry about taxes. Alice thought to herself, "Where would I be if Tom White hadn't been the cop that arrested me?" She didn't have to think too long. She knew. The graveyard, the nut house or prison.

Anyway, the grapevine must still be working, because Old Poole was coming in the door.

"Hey, Alice, who got it, who's on it and what's it about?" Poole asked.

"Well Poole, let's see. Don't know who got it, Tom's on it, and don't know what it's about."

"Betcha Tom's got it boxed up in twenty-four hours, Alice."

"Poole, you always say that."

"Not always . . . do I?" Poole grinned.

"How about a cheeseburger, Poole? Are ya hungry?" Alice smiled.

"Now that you mention it, Alice, I'm starving. Okay, a cheeseburger, extra onions."

Poole was an ancient, retired cop, a real pain in the ass, but Alice was nice to him. He had nobody. Sometimes she worried that he'd swallow his gun. Not today, anyway.

Chapter Two

Tom called in on the homicide. It was at 510 Maryland Street, not the best of neighborhoods, even for a city like Camden. Tom asked if the Coroner had been called. They told him Dan Gross would meet him there. Tom always thought how well Dan's name matched his job, but Dan was probably the best forensics man in the state. Dan had been a professor at Rutgers University. Why Dan gave up a tenured job like that, for this, made Tom wonder more than once. He was sure Dan had his reasons. Hell, everyone had to have a reason or think they did to work in a city called one of America's Worst on some TV show. What was it? Sixty Minutes or PBS? What the hell's the difference.

"What do ya think, Dwayne, gang territory, isn't it?"

"Yeah, some dealer probably came up short last night and got demoted to the graveyard. Probably some sixteen-year-old genius that was trying to buy a Lexus for his seventeenth birthday."

"Yeah," Tom said, "the sad thing is, one in a hundred does it and that's all the young bloods see. They don't see the other ninety-nine because forty-nine of them are in jail, and Dan Gross probably has the other fifty in the morgue."

"Saturday nights are hell in Camden," Dwayne remarked.

Tom drove fast, but not too fast. He knew to watch for open manholes. The junkies scrapped this area of the city so completely, that the only metal left was the sewer covers on the manholes, and lately, they'd been going fast.

Tom grabbed the radio, called the shop to tell them to pick up a junkie who was really looking bad at the corner of Federal and Fourth. Junkies weren't really that bad when they had their junk. But when they hit the last bag that they could beg, borrow or steal, they just fell apart. Well, this guy was there.

Filthy, one shoe, shit his pants and his face was bleeding. Skinny as a rail. Must have the Big "A". The radio squawked. Squad was on the way for the junkie.

Tom said, "Thanks, hope it will help him."

They turned off Federal onto Maryland.

"Did you see that?" Dwayne asked, amazed.

"Yeah," Tom said, "but I don't believe it. I've never seen a cab down here. He's lost or new, but I guarantee you, if he gets back to Federal Street with his wallet, he'll never come down here again."

"I bet the junkie doesn't have the only shitty pants on this block," Dwayne said, pointing to the cab.

Tom laughed a healthy laugh. In spite of his overweight looks, he was healthy and strong as a bull. Dwayne noticed that. Dwayne noticed a lot. He didn't know it, but that's why Tom had asked the Captain to use Dwayne until Sugar was back. Tom knew this city and he knew that having a black partner was good business, but having a smart partner was even better. Sugar and Dwayne were both smart.

"Dwayne, look for a number on that door."

"Hell, Tom, there are no doors. Let me count up from the corner, 500, 502, 504, empty lots, 506, 508, 510. Pull over. What the fuck? A homicide and nobody's here yet? This is it."

"This stinks," Tom said. "Somebody ought to be here. Who called this in?"

Dwayne asks, "Are we going in?"

"Not unless you've got a big "S" on your chest. I'll call the shop."

"No "S" on my chest, and I know I ain't Superman. Call it in." Dwayne agreed.

"Hold on, what's this going on, Tom?" Dwayne asked.

"It's Peter and Paul. What the hell are they doing? It looks like they're fighting. They are fighting! At least Peter is! Pull up there."

"Yo, Yo, Yo, break it up. What the fuck is this?" Tom demanded.

Paul was out of breath. Peter looked bad, not beaten up. Shock! Peter was in shock. Tom had seen panic attacks before and this one was a beauty.

Dwayne jumped from the car, and ran the thirty feet to Peter and Paul. Tom thought how fast he was.

"Help me with him," Paul said.

Dwayne grabbed Pete in a bear hug. He was soaked to the skin. Paul, relieved, fell back on the squad car.

Tom walked over; "I want to know what's going on!" Then, he got a good look at Pete.

"Dwayne, see if you can get him into the car."

"Paul, you okay?" Tom asked.

"I guess so, Lieutenant," Paul gasped.

"Good, call an ambulance for your partner."

"Dwayne, how is he?" asked Paul.

"Soaked, dilated, heart beating like a drum. What's going on? He was okay at the Lantern fifteen minutes ago." Dwayne said.

"Fifteen minutes can be a lifetime. Is that unit on the way?"

"It'll be here any minute, Sir," Paul said.

"Were you in there? In 510?"

"Yes, Sir," Paul said. "We both were. Pete lost it and just bolted. I jumped in the car and caught him on Indiana."

"Hell, that's three blocks away," Tom said.

"I know and he covered it in less than a minute. If he hadn't fallen, he'd still be running. It was murder trying to get him into the car."

"It's that bad?" the Lieutenant asked.

"Oh, yeah, it's that bad." Paul sobbed.

"Okay, okay, take it easy. We'll get everything straightened out. Sit in the car. Call for a backup unit. I want you to drive to the station. Can you drive?"

"I can drive. I'll be okay, just give me a minute, Sir. I'm a good cop. A damn good cop, just give me a minute." Paul was crying.

Tom knew Paul was a good cop; ten years worth of good cop, in a bad city. He'd seen a lot. Tom had a real bad feeling. He felt that this was going to be one of those days that kept you from sleeping, eating and loving.

The ambulance pulled to the curb for Peter. Dwayne said something to the driver. Peter got in. Tom had to wonder how many more rides in an ambulance this day would demand.

"Lieutenant, I'm all right," Paul said, rubbing his face.

"You sure?"

"Yeah, yeah, I mean, yes Sir."

"Calm down and remember, it's just 'Tom' out here."

Dwayne was with the Lieutenant now. They looked at each other. They looked at Paul.

"Jesus, get me that job in the DA's office," Dwayne said.

"Maybe you're right about that," Tom whispered as he passed Dwayne.

"Well, let's go in," Tom said.

As they were about to enter the house, a couple of squatters, aroused from their stupor, shouted. "What's the racket?"

Paul wheeled toward them. "Shut the fuck up and get the fuck out of here. I see you're fucking face one more time, you're going to jail, dirt ball." The squatters ducked back into the hovel.

Tom said, "Officer, I couldn't have said that better myself. Everything considered."

Paul almost laughed. Dwayne did. That was why Tom White was so good. He could loosen up when the situation called for it. Right now, he knew Paul needed to blow some steam or just vent some good, old fashioned, anger.

They entered the building, a thin row home. These houses were once the pride of the city. Now they were the plague.

"Tom, I've got a light, you'll need it." Paul said.

"Thanks, where?" Tom asked.

"End of the hallway, down the stairs. Watch it! A couple steps are missing," Paul added.

Dwayne took the light and led the way. Tom followed. Paul brought up the rear.

Dwayne shined the light down the stairs and started down. Tom stopped at the top.

"Do you smell that?" Tom asked.

Dwayne replied, "I smell it, it's perfume."

"It gets stronger," Paul said.

Dwayne was slowly moving down the stairs. "Watch the steps," he warned. "The fourth and fifth are missing."

The basement was two small rooms. The room at the bottom of the steps was unremarkable. Well, unremarkable for this city. The floor was littered with trash, old unrecognizable, wet and rotting rags, newspaper someone had used for toilet tissue, empty forty ounce beer bottles, Philly Blunt cigar wrappers. The cigars had long since been loaded with pot and smoked by some loser in this Shangri La.

Tom said, "Paul, go outside and rip some wood or siding off the house and hand it down to Dwayne."

"Right, Boss," Paul was gone.

"Dwayne, when Paul comes back, hand me down the wood, I'll make a path. I'm not stepping in this shit. Hell, these shoes are brand new."

Dwayne followed Paul's path back up the stairs. He knew Tom wanted an uninterrupted moment to get the feel of the place. Tom always talked about "feel". Dwayne didn't second-guess Tom. Nobody did. Tom got results, usually. He was usually right and pretty fast about it.

Tom shined the light through the dark room. The combination of sweet perfume and sour smells was sickening. The air was truly putrid. At the end of the room hung a curtain or a sheet. It was white, whatever it was. The whiteness of it was such a contrast to the washed out room, that when the light shown on it, Tom was forced to squint.

"Dwayne, you there?"

"Yeah, Tom."

"Pass me down whatever you got . . . nails?" he asked.

"A couple, but they're flattened." Dwayne passed down the lumber.

Tom took the first piece and carefully laid it on the trash-covered floor. He moved out onto the lumber. Slowly, he moved to the end.

"Okay, Dwayne, come down. I'll need one more board that long, you got it?"

"Yeah." Dwayne called, "Paul, pass me that longer one, any nails?"

Paul passed it to Dwayne, "No nails."

Dwayne moved down the stairs. "No nails," he said as he passed the board to Tom.

Tom thought how little things like checking boards for nails, drove him nuts, when he was a rookie. Twenty years later, he knew a nail could be as deadly as a bullet in a filthy spot like this. Tetanus had sickened more than one careless officer and killed a few good K-9's.

Tom laid out the board. It reached the curtain. He walked to the curtain. The stench . . . sticky-sweet. The smell brought to mind one of the whores he'd busted on the Admiral Wilson Boulevard at the end of a very successful night's work.

"Dwayne, work your way over to me. You got the camera ready?"

"With film and light, ready to roll."

"Paul," Tom yelled.

"Yeah," Paul replied.

"I want you out front. Wait for the other unit and nobody comes down here but Dan Gross, and I mean nobody."

"You got it, Boss," Paul answered with an equal measure of relief and gratitude.

"Dwayne, no matter what's in there, I want that camera to roll. Cover me and whatever I'm looking at. No sorry ass lawyer from Cherry Hill is going to be talking about contaminated evidence on this one. You okay?" Tom thought Dwayne looked shaky.

"I'm good, Tom. I guess I'm just anxious."

"If you weren't anxious now, I'd have to write you up for an evaluation. Get right behind me, camera rolling, now."

"The film's rolling," Dwayne said.

Tom removed from inside his jacket, an extendible wand that he always carried. He opened it and raised it to move the white cloth.

"Satin," he mumbled. "The sheet is satin."

"Dwayne, this sheet is brand new satin. It must have cost a few bucks. Weird."

"All right, I'm opening the curtain."

Tom glanced back at Dwayne. Dwayne was steady.

"Okay, do it," Dwayne said. "I'm filming."

Tom turned back to the scene. It was carnage. He stood still, just staring.

"Jesus wept," Tom said.

"How long's Pete been on the force?" he asked.

"A little over two years, Boss."

"If I were him, I would have bolted, too."

The small room was draped in bright white satin . . . the wall, ceiling and floor. The body was horrific. It was a woman. The flesh, from the waist down, was gone. The upper torso was fully fleshed.

Tom stepped back, still holding the curtain open. He needed air. Perfume hammered his nostrils. He put his tie across his face.

"Dwayne, get it together. I know you can do it."

Dwayne was shaking. So was Tom, but Tom wasn't holding the camera.

"Dear God, dear God, oh Lord," Dwayne mumbled.

"You're okay, right?"

"As okay as anyone could be, I guess," Dwayne answered.

Tom knew Dwayne was right. How the hell could he be okay? Tom turned back to the chamber. He had been in Vietnam and seen many bad things, but this . . . .

"You got sound?" Tom asked.

"Got it," Dwayne said.

"The corpse is a woman, age thirty to forty, hair blonde, height can only be guessed as average. Legs are too mutilated to be sure. It looks like something has been fashioned from the skin and tissue, to simulate a baby suckling at the breast. The object has been sewn to the body of the victim. Crudely, but with many heavy stitches, one about every quarter inch around the entire figure."

He continued. "The victim's mouth has been sewn tightly shut, as well as the eyes and nose. Someone was here for a long time."

"The room is covered with satin, and at the woman's head are two bouquets of flowers, one red roses and one, lilies. There is what appears to be a new bicycle standing next to the body. It has pink and white streamers, a girl's bike. There's a card on the bike. Three words, 'For your birthday.' No signature. The floor is covered with traces of someone walking or kneeling all around the body. There's a bottle of, it looks like, perfume, with a basin and a blood-soaked rag on the floor. Blood is splashed on the white satin drapes covering most of the walls."

"This is Lieutenant Tom White. I'm backing out of the scene now. Filming is by Sergeant Dwayne Cherry, Camden City Police Force. The time is 1:04 PM, Sunday, July 26, 1998."

"Back up, Dwayne."

Dwayne, camera still rolling, backs up, slowly. Tom lets the curtain fall.

"Cut the camera, Dwayne."

"Hey Tom, you ready for me?" Dan Gross called.

Tom recognized his voice, but said nothing. He waved Dwayne to retreat to the stairs. He was dripping wet, so was Dwayne. As they climbed the stairs, Tom had trouble where the steps were missing. Dwayne reached down to offer him a hand.

"Hell, I had trouble myself and I'm twenty years younger than you are," Dwayne admitted.

Tom took Dwayne's hand and was pulled up the stairs. Tom felt Dwayne's hand shaking. He felt his own legs shaking.

At the top of the stairs, they paused. Looking at his watch Tom said, "Two hours ago, your wife was waving goodbye to us. Seems impossible."

Dwayne agreed. "Yeah, almost like it were other people, somebody on film or in a book."

Dan Gross was in his gear, all of it. Lab coat, full apron, skullcap, mask ready to cover his face, gloves and boots. Shelly King, his ever faithful and trusted assistant was with him. Shelly was one good-looking girl. Hell, she's not a girl anymore, but she was when Tom first met her four years ago. Now, he realized she was a woman. Why now, he wondered? Maybe because she was blonde, like the woman downstairs. Tom got a chill. Shelly was built like Linda Hamilton, in the second Terminator movie. Tom knew her mind and body were a perfect match. More than one creep had found out the hard way when they had tried to interfere with the Coroner. He knew she was more than Dan's assistant. She was his bodyguard.

Tom had been to dinner with Shelly and Dan more than a few times. He'd thought of asking her for a date, she seemed to like him, but he was old fashioned and more importantly, twice her age. Tom knew her grandmother had been one of the survivors of Sobibor. Dan had told him. If her grandmother was anything like Shelly, she was probably the driving force behind the breakout at the famous prison. Shelly against a Nazi? No contest! Ninety-nine times out of a hundred, Shelly would win that one.

Still, in the right setting, she was sweet, even gracious at times. She brought to mind the women of Jane Austin's novels that Tom was so fond of, but never spoke about.

"Dan, how did you know it would be a bad one? I see you brought all your gear," Tom asked.

"Well Tom, I looked at Officer Clark when I arrived and just started strapping up."

"Yeah, I should've guessed. Hi, Shelly."

"Hi, Tom," Shelly answered. "Hi, Dwayne."

"Dan, Shelly, try to get us something to go on here. We've got to get this creep fast," Dwayne said.

"We always do try, Dwayne," Dan answered.

"I'm sorry. I know. I know you two are the best. It's just that . . . I don't know . . . I'm all shook up. I'll get this film to the car. I gotta sit down."

"Tom, he's worried, I think his tie was crooked," Shelly smiled.

Dwayne was known for his good looks and sharp clothes. He was always the best-dressed man in the crowd. More than once, someone asked him for his autograph, thinking he was one of the 76er's.

"Shelly, Dwayne's right to be worried. Whoever did this took his time, and I think he liked his work. He must have been down there for hours. I was there about thirty minutes and it was all I could stand."

"What do you want, Tom?" Shelly asked.

She was like a racehorse in the gate. "God, she was tough," he thought.

"Everything . . . entire contents of the room, photos, prints, dental . . . we've got nothing to go on. I want the flowers, the bike, everything to go to the lab."

"Flowers! Shit, I'd go out with this guy if he's handing out flowers." Shelly laughed.

"Shelly!" Dan admonished.

Shelly struck a pose like her feelings were hurt. Tom and Dan both had to chuckle.

"I'd better get her down there, Tom, before she pushes me down the stairs," Dan said.

"Oh hell, the stairs. Shelly, two stairs are missing. Dan might have a problem with his bad leg."

"No sweat. I'll use a bone saw to trim some scrap. Take me two minutes."

Shelly smiled and went to work now, as Dan's carpenter.

"Dan, can you tell me one thing that girl cannot do?" Tom asked.

"Yes, I can," he grinned.

"And that is?"

"Relax."

Tom said, "I'll leave you both to it. I've got to call the Captain, and he's not going to like it."

"That's right. Today's the big to do at the Aquarium. Is he still trying to get the Texas money men to build on the RCA lot?"

"Damn right! If they told him the only project they had in mind was a fifteen-story whorehouse, I think he'd go for it," Tom joked.

"I'll stop by the lab about six. I might bring Shelly flowers," Tom laughed.

"Tom, she'd like that. See you at six."

Tom turned quickly, walking to Dwayne. Dwayne was back on top of his game. His ability to quickly manage men and material were the best Tom had seen since he'd been on the force. He had a pair of officers out front. Nobody was getting in. There were two officers at each end of the street. Along with Willis Taylor's imposing figure, Dwayne was knocking at the door of a house that looked like the only legitimate property on the street.

Dwayne noticed Tom and held up a finger, meaning he'd be over in a minute.

Tom asked a young cop, who was smoking, for a cigarette and a light. The rookie obliged. Tom's first smoke in two months and that first drag was like Mother's Milk.

"How the hell can you quit smoking in this goddamn city?" he thought.

As he smoked, Tom wondered why Dan had told him that Shelly would like flowers. Was he joking or was there something else in it?

When it came to a crime, Tom was a whiz. When it came to women, he had the aplomb of a schoolboy. Tom dated now and then, but he wasn't able to separate his job from his life and this turned off the women he had known.

"Christ," he thought, "how can you see the things you see in this toilet and walk into a home and say, 'Hi, honey, what's for dinner? Have we got anything on tonight? Movie, dancing, cards with the neighbors?'"

Tom liked to go home and listen to the guys bitch about the Phillies and the Eagles on the AM sports station. It was the only radio station where you could be sure you wouldn't hear any crap about crime, or some sobbing mother begging for help to find her missing kid, or worse.

There was a guy named Howard on that station. Tom thought what a great job he had. Every time someone called in with a stupid comment, Howard would say, "You're stupid and you're off the air." What a great job! An asshole pops up, you cut him off. Tom had assholes up to his eyelids, and they weren't going anywhere.

Speaking of which, he'd call the Captain about five and fill him in. He'd be done kissing ass by then. For Pete's sake, any moron could figure out it would be a long time before any outside money came into this town.

Tom finished his smoke. He didn't know why, but it had made him sad to crush it out. Where's Dwayne? He looked down the street. Maybe he's got something.

Tom thought about going down to see how Dan was making out, but he decided against it. He realized they didn't need his help and Shelly would probably tell him to beat it. She was famous for that. Nobody interrupted Dan when he was at work, if she could help it, and she usually could. She once told Captain Mel Tracy to get his fat ass out of the house, when she thought he was crowding Dan for some fast answers. Answers didn't come fast in this line of work and even the Captain must have known that. The Captain swore he'd get Shelly fired. He called Dan to tell him she was done. Dan told the Captain that aside from the fact that she was the best assistant money could buy, money couldn't buy her. Shelly was a full time volunteer. Four years, sixty hours a week and she hadn't been paid a dime. Dan wanted to know how the Captain was going to explain firing a highly motivated, Princeton educated woman, who worked sixty hours a week for no salary. It would take two full time employees to replace her at the cost of about a hundred thousand a year and both of them wouldn't be the equal of Shelly, even if they could find two people who wanted her grizzly job. The Captain was a jackass, but he wasn't a fool. So Tracy told Dan to try and keep her on a damn leash when he was around. The Captain ended this conversation by telling Dan he'd come to any crime scene he chose when he felt his presence was required. That was over a year ago and Dan and Shelly hadn't seen Mel's fat ass since. Anyway, Tom knew he just wanted to be near Shelly. Thinking about it, he felt a little foolish.

Dwayne appeared at Tom's shoulder.

Tom jumped a bit when Dwayne said, "Great gifts come in small packages."

"Someone saw the actor?" Tom asked excitedly.

"No, she didn't see anything over here." Dwayne smiled.

"Then why the grin, Mr. Ultrabright?" Tom cracked. Dwayne had the whitest teeth he had ever seen and he was a little self-conscious about his own teeth. Oh, he had them all, but after smoking for thirty years, at best they could be described as light gray.

Dwayne grinned, savoring the moment.

"In that little detached row home, lives one Maria Antoinette Gonzales," Dwayne paused, dusting his jacket.

Oh, he's loving this, Tom thought. Dwayne knew he had no patience and this act could only mean something really sweet.

"Dwayne, would you like to keep that Hollywood smile?" Tom asked.

"All right, all right, cool it." Dwayne mocked fear and backed off a yard from Tom.

"Here it is. Willis is knocking on the few doors that this block has. Right? We get the standard responses . . . No savvy, no savvy . . . Rottweilers barking . . . the regular, then we knock on Maria's door."

"Maria's door? What are you, old friends?" Tom asked.

"I was in there long enough, and the way she talks, I feel comfortable calling her Maria."

"All right, I shouldn't have said that, I admit it. Please continue."

"Maria opens the door without even asking who's there. That's strange behavior down here. We asked her if she saw anything across the street here? Right away she starts with the 'Come in, come in, sit down, have coffee'."

"I say 'No, thanks,' but you know Willis. He chimes right in that he'd love a cup, extra cream and six sugars."

"She heads for the kitchen and I'm looking around in shock. That dumpy looking house is a small palace inside and I'm not joking. Remember the old Latin Casino out on Route 70? Well, the floor survived or at least a portion of it, because it's in there, logo and all. The letter "L" with the laurel kudos in brass surrounding it, inlaid in green Italian marble, is now the floor of that house. The entire first floor, front to back, living room, dining room and kitchen all done in green marble. Willis used the powder room behind the kitchen, same floor he told me."

Dwayne continues, "Aside from the wide screen television and killer sound system, the walls are done in a light pink plaster, with sculpted cornices. It's a real plaster job, not a knock off like you get at the local hardware megastore. The furniture is Italian leather sectional, soft as buttermilk. The stairs are glass block, three inches thick. Rails are brass and real well done. From what

I observed, I would guess it took three hundred thousand to fix that place up."

Tom raised his eyebrows and looked over at the shabby house. It was hard to believe. The place fit the neighborhood perfectly. It was a dump.

"So what's her story? She win the lottery and make some contractor rich, or what?"

Dwayne smiled, "Definitely, or what. I told her what a nice place it was. She thanked me and told me her son Hernan had it done for her. He was a doctor. I asked if she saw anything across the street last night."

She said, "Si, El Diablo."

I asked her if she would mind explaining that and she said, "He's still there, look out the window. You can see for yourself."

"I looked at her closely and realized she did have a cracked look about her. I glanced out the window. El Diablo had vanished. I wasn't surprised. I told her I could get him to move to another neighborhood. She was genuinely grateful. Hell, she came across the room and kissed me. Willis got up and excused himself. He was trying not to bust up laughing."

"Anyway, here's the punch line. I get up, trying to leave, she's pawing me, she's so grateful that I'm going to rid her of El Diablo. By the door, on her baby grand piano, there's a picture that catches my eye. I comment on what a handsome man is in the picture."

"Oh," she says. "Thank you, that is my Hernan."

"The doctor?" I ask.

"Yes," she says. "He does everything for me."

"Well here it is; the picture, it's Mag."

Tom jumped off the hood of the car. "No shit!"

"Swear to God," Dwayne says. "No wonder we could never find his larder."

"You found it?" Tom said.

"Oh, yeah. I told her my father was a doctor, too, and our house was always filled with his supplies," Dwayne chuckled. "Right off, she says 'my house, too'. Just look up here."

"She takes me upstairs. We open the back bedroom door and wham! There it is. Must be a hundred pounds of coke, and there's weed stacked to the ceiling. A sign hangs there. Medical Supplies for Puerto Rico. Do Not Touch Mama."

"Good work, you lucky bastard. We can watch that house from here. You go get a warrant. You were invited in?"

"Absolutely."

"Fucking great." Tom watched Dwayne jog to the car. "Hey, hold up," he yelled.

Tom walked over to meet Dwayne. "Dwayne, does Willis know?"

Dwayne took a quick look Willis's way. "No."

"Good, let's keep this between me, you and Judge Bisbing."

"You got doubts about Willis?" Dwayne asked.

"No, not at all, but if he knew, everybody would know. He's got a big mouth."

"Ah, hell, I knew that," Dwayne said.

"That's the only reason I asked. Now, take off, Tiger."

Tom turned back toward the crime scene. He wondered how long he would have to live with this mess.

"El Diablo," he thought, "Maria could have seen him. This was most definitely the work of the devil, but he was gone now."

The body was on a stretcher, now. Two officers were helping with the plastic bags full of satin sheets and blood. Another loaded the bike, now wrapped in plastic, also.

"Dan, is that it?"

"That's everything," Dan said. "What time is it, Tom?"

"Almost three."

"See you at six. I'll let you know what we've got. Don't eat, we'll try Rexy's for some pizza."

"I don't think I'll be eating tonight, but I'll go for a few beers. I need one," Tom said.

"After all these years, still squeamish." Dan said.

"Anchovies for me." Shelly chimed in.

Tom shook his head, turning away. "Six o'clock."

Shelly smiled as she walked toward the van with Dan. She liked to needle Tom. He was such an easy target.

Tom called everybody in; the cop in him knew they'd be ready to go.

"Look, anybody got anything to add to what we already know?" Tom asked.

The cops looked at each other, then looked at Tom. They were hot and bored and he knew it.

"Okay guys, thanks a lot. Look, one more thing. Whip the blocks around here for about five minutes. See if you can get a runner, maybe we can still shake something up. Okay, beat it."

"Okay Lieutenant," Willis said.

"Willis, who are you with," Tom asked?

"Terry Davis."

"Terry, take the car up by the Speed Line." Tom smiled. "When Gormley comes by, tell him it's yours for the rest of the shift. Oh yeah, is your air working?"

"The air is working, Sir. I'm outta here."

Willis's smile was a mile wide watching Terry leave.

Tom smiled at Willis. "You think that's real funny, don't you Willis?"

"Well, I do have a good sense of humor. When I tell Ready you gave Speed Line Sunday to a black rookie, that cracker is going to have a goddamn stroke. He down on Kaighn all goddamn day. Son of a bitch must look like a kernel of corn in a bowl of baked beans." Willis slapped both his hands on top of the cruiser and roared with laughter.

Tom had to turn away to keep from busting up himself.

"Hey man, hold up a minute," Tom called to a young kid walking down the street.

"How old are you, son?"

The kid turned his left shoulder toward Tom. Standard defense position for a right handed kid. "Fourteen, Dude, why?"

"Then you're too young to smoke. Give me those smokes in your pocket." Tom said.

"Hey man, they my mom's."

Tom grabbed the smokes. He opened the pack. "You always take your mom's last three smokes for a walk?"

"You fucked up man," the kid said.

"Beat it," Tom replies.

The kid was pissed, but looking over Tom's shoulder he saw Willis's 6'5", 410 pound frame and turned to start walking.

"Yo, dude," Tom called.

The kid turned around. "What you want now, my fucking matches?"

Tom laughed and tossed a green ball to the kid. The kid caught it and straightened it out.

"Yo, man, you cool, you too cool. Later."

The kid started walking away with a kick in his step.

"What'd you give him?" Willis asked.

"A twenty. Hell, it's the end of the month. His family can see the Colonel tonight."

"Shit! No way is he gonna take that home." Willis said.

"Leave me my illusions," Tom said. "He looks like a good kid."

"Softy," Willis smiled.

"Well, Willis, let's wait five minutes. If Dwayne doesn't call me, we'll go. You got anything in that flask of yours?"

"You know about that, huh?"

"I know my men, but I'm just guessing."

Willis produced a chrome hip flask. "I only carry this as a bullet stopper. I keep having a dream that I get shot in the hip."

Tom took the flask, just as the kid without the smokes, but with the twenty, was at the corner. The kid yelled, "Yo, Yo, Yo."

Tom and Willis both looked his way.

"Yo! I would have kicked your white ass 'cept for the fact you got that fat ass grizzly bear behind you, Whitebread," the kid yelled.

As the kid vanished, Willis laughed, "Oh hell, yes. I can see him buying Colonel Sanders for the whole family tonight."

"You drive, Willis. No, hold up. I need somebody here tonight. I'll need two good men."

"Back to the scene of the crime theory?" Willis asked.

"No, this wacko isn't coming back here. He completed his work, but look over at the Gonzales house."

Willis looked over Tom's shoulder. "Don't tell me you could feel her peeking out of that window?"

"She is, isn't she?"

"Yeah, she is. You white folks are spooky."

"Not really. I see her reflection in the window behind your back," Tom smiled.

"You figure she might have been peeping and maybe this guy thinks she could have seen something?" Willis asks.

"Right the first time, Grizzly Taylor."

"Yeah, maybe. Who do you want?"

"Well they better be young and Spanish or light skinned."

"Tom, how about Rosa and Jesus. I know they're doing Sting, but on Sunday, the Parade is slow."

"Perfect, you get in touch with them. Eleven to seven ought to be good. This guy works at night. No sense keeping them here any longer than that. Tell them that if anybody goes into that house, I want to know."

"When I was in there, I looked around pretty good. I don't think she gets much company, seems lonely." Willis added.

"All right. Let's beat it, then all the nice people can come out and play."

"You got my flask," Willis stuck out his hand.

"It's all yours. I didn't even use it."

"You're luckier than you know. That's my uncle's South Carolina Corn."

"Thanks for the warning, Willis."

"I wonder who she was?" Tom thought out loud.

"Don't wonder, Tom. Spinning your wheels will just tear you up. Dan might know soon. Let it go for now."

Willis turned up Federal Street and headed downtown. He looked at Tom. Tom was looking at the radio.

"What are you waiting to hear from Dwayne about?" Willis asked.

"Trying to find the owner of that house. He's probably down the basement going through the old records."

"Damn, Tom, he'll be pissed."

"Why's that?"

"Probably get dusty," Willis chuckled.

"There's no radio down there, if there was I'd call him," Tom said.

"Did Dwayne tell everyone not a word to anyone on this?"

"In no uncertain terms, Lieutenant."

"Good, but you know, he's the only one I'm worried about. He's got a big mouth."

"Ah hell, I know that," Willis smiled.

Tom smiled, too and lit up a cigarette.

Chapter Three

Tom pulled into Rexy's. The lot was about half full. If it were November or any other cooler month, you'd be lucky to find a spot to park. But in July, in South Jersey, all the people who wanted to dine out went to the Shore. Tom couldn't blame them. The Jersey Shore was loaded with great restaurants. No better than Rexy's, but Rexy's had no beach or boardwalk. The Shore also had another draw. Atlantic City's casinos.

Twenty years ago, gambling had come to Atlantic City and the people followed. Tom didn't understand gamblers. Didn't anybody else watch Westerns? Didn't they know the deck was stacked against them? He had a friend on the force in A.C. He told Tom that the suicide rate was four times what it had been before gambling came to town. Nobody ever heard about it. Money has a way of keeping things quiet and in Jersey, money was king. Tom had read the local papers many times expecting to find a story or someone he knew or had been personally involved with, who had committed suicide, but not a line. Tom thought if someone from California was looking to relocate and read every South Jersey paper for a year, they'd think that aside from a few highly publicized murder cases, and a couple of D.W.I.'s, this was the greatest place in the world. Tom knew better, much better.

Tom knew that the news blackout didn't stop with the newspapers. The local television stations showed traffic jams and house fires every night. Oh, yeah! A really big story was a busted water main across the river in Philadelphia. Some poor son of a bitch's basement got flooded. Always the victim, in front of the cameras. "I've got no insurance, boo hoo, and look, my kid's teddy bear got wet."

Tom used to get pissed. He thought to himself, "Why don't they bring in a film crew to Mt. Ephraim Avenue on Friday night, around ten o'clock. They could film the parade. Couldn't do that. They might see some rich kid going slumming for drugs, and that could ruin a good round of golf. Heck, the station manager might even lose some good advertising.

Back to the money, it's always about the damn money.

The "parade" . . . what a damn shame he thought. Every Friday and Saturday night, the kids came from all the local small towns to Camden to get their drugs. Coke, heroin, weed, crack or whatever else is popular at the time. Bumper to bumper traffic into one of the worst neighborhood's in a bad city, and usually, not a cop in sight.

Oh, the cops were there. You just couldn't see them. They worked the druggies on the way into town in unmarked cars. On the way out of town, they stopped them in black and whites.

It was like swatting mosquitoes at the Shore with a land breeze blowing out of the Pine Barrens. There were just too many to swat. Once in a while there would be a big deal in the papers about an open-air drug market being shut down. There were forty or fifty of these impromptu bazaars. The drug market was like crab grass. You just couldn't kill it. Tom realized that even this, was still, just about money. He didn't think about it much anymore. It was too depressing.

"Jesus, this case is getting me down already," Tom realized, as he fired up a Marlboro. Was it really just two days since he was at the beach with Zach, his brother Sam's kid? Thinking of Zach was helping. Zach was a happy, handsome eight-year-old. Tom liked spending time with him. The kid made him laugh and he knew, when a cop couldn't laugh, he was in deep trouble.

Tom checked his Timex Indiglo, a cheap watch that never failed. It was eight forty-five. He had stopped by the Lab at six, gotten some tidbits from Dan. At seven, Shelly told him he didn't look good. Well, he didn't feel good.

Shelly said, "Just go. We'll meet you at Rexy's about nine."

He knew Shelly got a kick out of Tom's turning green at the Lab. It didn't happen most of the time, but this one was way off the gruesome scale, especially since it was a woman. Tom had been in Vietnam. He'd seen lots of corpses, but hell, over there, you expected it. The cases involving women were always shocking to him, probably because he was so close to his mother and sister. He never really spent a lot of time outside of school with boys, when he was growing up. His father was racing dirt track up in Mercer County and was killed when he was five. It hit his mother hard. She never remarried.

Tom lit a smoke. The air was cooler now as the night deepened. He pulled down the visor in his Jeep Cherokee and looked in the mirror. He studied his face. He liked his looks. He wondered how he would be described if he were the object of a manhunt. Let's see! The subject is male, Caucasian, great head of black hair, green eyes, good nose, square jaw, a good tan, six feet tall, two hundred pounds. Much like Mel Gibson, only better.

"Jesus," he thought, "I've got to get my teeth bleached."

Well, if he ever did cross that line, nobody described your teeth.

Nine o'clock. They were going to be late.

A car came into the lot and parked next to Tom. It wasn't them. Tom bent down to pick up an extreme sports magazine that Zach had left on the floor.

Bang! "Wake up, and let's eat."

Tom jumped. "Jesus, Shelly, you want me to catch a heart attack?"

Tom could feel his face flush and his blood pumping. He realized he was relieved. He smiled. He should have guessed it was Shelly slamming the roof of the Jeep. She wouldn't miss an opportunity like that. It crossed Tom's mind that being married to Shelly would either keep you alive until you were a hundred or kill you in six months.

"I didn't think you had a heart. Let's go in. I could eat a horse. I wonder if horse is kosher?"

"You sneaky bitch. You got a new car."

"Yeah, you like it?"

"Gee whiz, who wouldn't? It must've cost you a year's pay. I forgot, you don't get paid."

"It was Angel's car, remember her?"

"Sure I do. How'd you get it?"

"At auction," she grinned. "It was her pimp's. He got blown away when the cops in Philly tried to serve him with a warrant for capping Angel. Ill gotten gains go to auction."

"It doesn't bother you that Angel was found in the trunk of that car?" Tom asked.

"I don't go in the trunk. I've got Triple A."

The hostess seated them. The waitress came and they ordered salads. Tom asked for a pitcher of Fosters, the Aussie beer.

They had a table overlooking the parking lot, which was one of the main reasons for eating here. The owner was smart. He realized people loved to eat looking out upon their cars. Tom looked out at Shelly's new car.

"You'll be all right as long as you keep your hair blonde."

"I thought about that, but what really marked that car as Angel's were the tags.

Tom laughed. "Oh yeah, 'Pussy'."

They both laughed. Tom realized how important having dinner with Shelly had become to him. He wondered if she felt the same.

"Should we order for Dan?" Tom asked.

"Why not," Shelly ordered spaghetti three times.

Tom didn't want pizza, anyway. Shelly's anchovies always put him off. She'd pick them off the pizza and drop them down her throat like Sylvester the Cat in the Tweety Bird cartoons. He knew she did it for effect. Again, he remembered how young she was.

"Well, it's nice to see you out with your daughter."

Tom looked up. "Stark," Tom said. "I hope you forgive me if I don't get up to shake your hand, you asshole."

Tom said very quietly, "We're about to eat here and you're face won't do a thing for my appetite."

"Is that the best you can do?" Stark smirked.

"I can do better. How about this. I get up and smell your breath to see if you've been drinking. Then, I call your parole officer and tell him you're drunk in a tavern."

"I was just leaving."

"Good, don't forget to pay your check."

"Who was that ugly son of a bitch?" Shelly asked.

"That's an old timer. He used to be a booky on the docks, but he's nobody anymore. He got a little excited when some little guy decided not to pay. Beat him to death with a bat in front of the wife and kids." Tom paused to watch Stark walk across the parking lot to the bus stop.

"He got life. Must be twenty-five years since I've seen him."

"Prison didn't do his looks any favors."

"Shelly, he always looked like somebody walked on his face with golf shoes. Hell, that may be why he was such a bad one. The hookers ran away from him, even when he was flush."

"Can't blame them for that. Ugly, ugly!"

"So . . . how's the car running?" Tom quickly asked, changing the subject.

"Smooth, very smooth Tom, it's only got eight thousand miles on it."

"Wow, it's new. I guess it is hard to drive when you're laying on your back. Shelly, do you mind saying what it went for? I mean shit, look at my Jeep. I'm gonna need wheels soon."

"Why would I mind telling you, you silly boy? My father got rich buying and selling. He was always proud of a sharp business deal and so anyone should be. Talking about money only embarrasses the people who don't have any."

"Yes," Tom smiled, "that would be me."

"Ha, ha, ha. Hey, that's right. I got it for fifteen thousand."

"Wow! What's the blue book?"

"Twenty seven. Sweet, huh?"

"I've got to get to that auction."

Glancing out the window, Shelly said, "Dan just pulled in."

"Right on time. Here's the food."

"Excuse me, Tom," Shelly left the booth.

Tom looked through the window. Shelly jogged across the lot to Dan's Lincoln. Man, it was good looking, but not half as good looking as Shelly's ass.

Shelly opened Dan's door and helped him out. Tom had noticed that Dan was having a little more trouble with his walking, lately. No wonder! A hip replacement two years ago and his leg never healed right after the accident last year. Tom figured that Dan had to be pushing seventy.

Tom waited impatiently, the food smelled great. "Where the hell are they?" he wondered.

Suddenly, he remembered Stark, and got up to walk outside, but they were coming through the door. Shelly didn't look happy. She slid into the booth next to Tom.

Dan would need most of the other bench. Dan wasn't fat, just large. Old men seemed to take up more room. There was Dan's cell phone, his paper, his hat, an umbrella, his pipe and tobacco, a large envelope and the briefcase . . . and this was what he carried in the summer.

"Unless there's something that needs our immediate attention, let's eat," Tom said.

Dan looked at Shelly, questioningly. Shelly said, "We can eat."

"Tom," Dan nodded.

"Evening, Dan," Tom returned.

They all dug in. It was great. A spoon could stand in the sauce for three seconds before it slowly leaned over. The cheeses were freshly ground. The Philadelphia area must be one of the best places to go Italian. Forget cheese steaks, they were for the tourists. Tom was mopping up his plate with some great Italian bread, when he realized no one had spoken a word for fifteen minutes. He hadn't, because his mouth was full. But this was very unusual for Dan and unheard of, for Shelly. He looked across to Dan, then over to Shelly.

"All right, let's talk," Tom said.

Shelly spoke first. "Dan says this is his last job."

Tom thought she was going to cry. "Professor Gross, is this true?" Tom couldn't believe it, but he thought he should have seen it coming.

Dan put his pipe in his hand to load it with Cherry blend. Tom reached for a smoke, too.

"Yes, it's true. I decided an hour ago."

"The leg's killing you, I can tell," Tom said.

"That's a small part of it. The larger parts are more important."

"Such as?" Tom asked.

"Where shall I start? First, I have to say this case has gotten to me. Second, the Captain was in the lab tonight, right after Shelly left. Lastly, it's just time."

Tom grinned, "I bet he waited for her to leave."

"He did. He said so. He said he wanted to talk to me alone."

"Yeah, right. The coward," Tom said.

Below a tear on Shelly's cheek, Tom noticed traces of a grin.

Dan puffed his pipe to a bright glow.

"What did he want?" Tom asked.

"That's what I want to know," Dan said. "He nosed around about this and that but he didn't really say anything. Something stinks, Tom. That gentleman, at the Lab on Sunday night? I never remember him doing that before. Are the Phillies playing tonight?"

"That's right," Tom said. "He should be there. He never misses a night game."

"For Pete's sake Dan, tell him."

"He wants to meet with you in the Mayor's office, tomorrow morning. You, Dwayne and the District Attorney."

"Something does stink, I agree with Dan," Shelly said.

"I've been in there before. So what's that got to do with you quitting?"

"Excuse me, Sir. I never quit anything. Let's call it a prompt retirement from the City."

"Oh, excuse me Dan, I didn't . . . ."

"Take it easy, Tom. I know how you feel about me. I feel more like a father to you than I do to my own sons." Dan smiled. "And Shelly . . ." Dan reached across to hold her hand.

Tom saw Dan's eyes water and Shelly was near sobbing.

"Well, we're a happy bunch," Tom choked out.

"Shut up, Tom," Shelly said.

"This is the perfect time to get to work," Tom tried to sound cheerful.

"You bet," Shelly said. "Nothing could hit me harder than this news has."

"Listen you two. It's time for me to go. I've always wanted to see Israel. I've got a brother in Tel Aviv and I'm going to live with him. Be happy for me."

"Hell Dan, I think that's great, but I'm going to miss you," Tom said.

"That's really great, Tom's right. I was thinking selfishly," Shelly smiled.

"Shelly, are you going to work with a new man?" Dan asked.

"No way! I decided two years ago that if you gave it up, I was done. I just couldn't work with anyone else."

"What will you do, Shelly?" Tom asked.

Tom could see that Shelly was upset, but he also knew she was happy for Dan. Heck, why wouldn't she be, he was getting away from here.

"Well, my gut tells me to follow Dan to Tel Aviv and get an apartment across the street from him. I could follow him around and see that he's okay. I know it sounds foolish, but you asked me."

Dan and Tom both had to laugh. Shelly laughed too.

"Shelly, believe it or not, I was worried about that," Dan smiled.

"I wouldn't be happy," Tom blurted out.

"You wouldn't?" Shelly asked.

"Damn it! I want you both to look at me and listen hard," Dan demanded.

"Tom, you are going to buy flowers, drive to Shelly's on Friday night, take her to dinner and a movie and if there's no good night kiss, I'll be really disappointed in you."

"Shelly, you are going to wear a dress and high heels and go out with Tom. I've been waiting for you to do this Tom, but I see that unless I kick you in the ass, you'll never say anything. I've never asked much of you two, outside of work related issues. I don't think this is too much."

Tom and Shelly both stared at Dan. Tom was flushed. Shelly looked pissed.

"Time is short in this world and I won't stand for anymore of this pussyfooting."

Dan laughed. He laughed hard.

"Do you two know there's a pool down at the station guessing when you two will go out? Everybody on the force knows you're crazy about each other." Dan looked at Tom and Shelly.

Tom looked at Shelly. She glared at Dan. Tom thought how pretty she was. He loved her angry face and this was a good one.

"Shelly, I'd like that," Tom said.

"If that's what Dan wants, okay."

"That's what I want, and don't look so shocked, Shelly. I should have said this two years ago," Dan smiled. "I apologize if I embarrassed anyone, but it had to be said. Now, let's forget it and get to work."

"Here or outside?" Shelly asked, still miffed.

"Outside, I'm not laying these photos out in a restaurant."

"Your car, in five minutes. I've got to go to the ladies." Shelly snapped.

"I'll get the check," Tom volunteered.

"Let me old friend, I'm leaving in a week. This is probably our Last Supper," Dan said.

"In a week!" Tom was shocked.

"I've been planning this for a while. I just didn't know how to tell Shelly."

"You're her world, Dan. I think it hit her pretty hard."

"You think I don't know that? Oy vey, I'm going to miss that woman. She is a woman, Tom, and you're no damn senior citizen. I think I know why you haven't asked her out. Well, shape up, dude. This is the nineties. There are a lot of couples out there that look a hell of a lot stranger."

Tom smiled at Dan, "Thanks for the kick in the ass."

"You're welcome."

Chapter Four

They walked to Dan's Lincoln. It was a beautiful evening. Tom had just enough Fosters to put a glow on things, but it wasn't only the beer that was creating the glow. Tom was thinking about Shelly. She did like him. Wow!

Dan and Tom were in no hurry to get in the car. The evening was nice.

"I always liked Lincolns," Tom said.

"That reminds me Tom, the car is yours."

"What?"

"It's yours."

"I couldn't take it, Dan. It wouldn't feel right."

"Oh, shut up, you sap. It's okay for you to buy groceries, every time you see somebody hard up. Tony's hot dog cart looks like it's doing a good business. He ever pay you back?"

"A little, his wife just had a baby. It's tough for him now."

"Tom, it's a tough city. You're not getting any younger. You've got to think of yourself."

"I'm all right," Tom said.

"You could be better. Hell man, you're too big hearted. What you've done for people over the years. I'm not saying your wrong, I'm just trying to say think of yourself more. Never mind, you're the way you are. I just worry about you."

"I'll try to do better, Dad."

"That's a good lad."

"Where's Shelly?" Tom asked.

"I'm sixty-eight and I still can't figure out what women do in the bathroom."

"Let me pay you something for the car."

"Tom, where would I park that thing in Tel Aviv? It wouldn't fit down half the streets. I'm pretty well off. Remember all that old furniture I had?"

"You had? You've already gotten rid of your furniture?"

"Months ago, anyhow I had an appraisal on the highboy in my bedroom . . . . eighty thousand. Those lamps I always complained about . . . forty thousand for the three of them. Tiffany's! Hell, I never knew it. My wife spent most of her time at flea markets and she must have known what she was doing. Those ugly vases behind the bar . . . over a thousand apiece. I know she didn't pay more than a couple of bucks for anything."

"Unbelievable, that's great."

"I wish I had spent more time with her. She was a great lady."

Tom didn't know what to say so he lit up a smoke.

Dan continued, "Anyhow, I've got plenty. I want you to have the car."

"Thanks Dan, I'll give Alice the Jeep."

"There you go again!"

They both laughed.

"What's so funny?" Shelly asked, as she walked over to the pair.

"Life," Dan answered. "But not the piece of it we have to talk about now. Everybody in."

Reviewing a case in the car was old hat. They learned a long time ago that it was the fastest way to get it completed. Sometimes they did this after a meal, inside the restaurant, if the place was nearly empty. At the station there were too many busybodies. There were also too many dumb questions, too many interruptions, and too many people looking to put their slant on things, for one of a dozen possible reasons. Like any big city force, there might be a rotten cop nosing around for his outside man. Their system of doing it in the car was the best way, tried and true and they were comfortable with it.

"Shelly, your pad, what we know," Dan said.

"Tom, yours, what we don't know."

"I'll scribe speculations."

This system worked. As evidence was examined, they found that if they each read what the other had taken down, it gave them a better picture of what had occurred and the type of perpetrator they were dealing with. They were a good team.

Dan laid his briefcase on the seat between himself and Tom. Shelly sat in the back, leaning over the front seat. Dan handed the envelope to Tom with a roll of masking tape.

"Those four should do it, Tom," Dan said, as he handed four photos to Tom.

Tom took the pictures without saying anything. He had done this so many times before. Tom taped the pictures so that they hung down the dashboard.

Shelly groaned. "I ate too much."

"That was my line, Shelly," Tom said.

"All right," Dan said, as he opened his briefcase. "This is what we know. Shelly do you have a pen?"

"Have pen!" Shelly said, all business now.

"What we know," Dan repeated. "One: The sheets were satin, expensive. Two: The bike was new, a young girl's, and expensive. Three: The sewing was done with heavy nylon thread. Four: The victim sat upon the bike, in a riding position, prints were found on the grips. Five: The amount of violence is extreme but very controlled. Six: The victim was heavily drugged. Heroin overdose. The drugs had been forced down her throat, undiluted. Seven: Wounds on her wrist show she had been restrained, recently. Eight: The flowers were two or three days old. Nine: Hairs found in the blood on the floor, the victim, and the satin sheets, contained all types of hair; black, Spanish, Caucasian, blonde, red, gray, wavy, curly, straight. The whole spectrum. Ten: The victim was an extremely good-looking female, healthy, clean, manicured and aside from the heroin, there were no other traces of drugs or alcohol. Eleven: She was never arrested as far as we can tell. Prints were negative. Twelve: She has perfect teeth, cleaned by a dentist or hygienist, recently. Thirteen: She was murdered and mutilated sometime between 10 p.m. Saturday and three a.m. Sunday. Fourteen: Chloroform odor still in body." Dan wiped his brow, "That's not much but it's a start."

"You need a break, Dan?" Tom asked.

"Let's keep going, it's past my bedtime."

"I'll start our 'Don't Know' list, okay Tom?" Shelly asked.

"Shoot," Tom replied.

Shelly leaned against the back seat and pushed her bare feet over the seat between the men. Tom thought to himself, "Even her feet look good." He tried to remember how long it had been since he had been with a woman. It must've been a long time because he honestly couldn't remember.

"One: Who was she? Two: Why the satin? Three: Why the bike? Four: Why the card? Dan, I'll put the card on the "Do Know" list when I'm through this.

"That's right, I missed that," Dan said.

Five: Why the flowers? Six: The hair seems like an obvious cover up tool, but I still want it on the 'don't know' for origin. Seven: We don't know what time, how and who got her into that shitty basement. Eight: The mutilation reason is either personal, sport, artistic or a contract killing, made to look like a psycho, but that's really unlikely. That's speculation. I guess I'm done. I know there's more ground to cover on the 'don't know' but I'm coming up dry," Shelly admitted.

"Your 'don't know' sounds good to me, Shelly, how about you, Dan?" Tom asked.

"Good enough for today, anyway," Dan said. "Speculations, Tom, your turn."

"Well, Dan, One: He knew her. Two: Once he thought he loved her. Three: She probably thought they were still friends. Four: She aborted his child or at least, a child. It screams this fact. Five: One time crime. Six: I think he got what he came for; satisfaction of a real or imagined wrong. Seven: He's either really big or really strong."

"How much did she weigh, Dan?" Tom asked.

"Let me see," Dan looked at the envelope.

"She weighed one hundred and forty pounds," Shelly said. Women always remember the weight.

"As I said, he must be very strong. The bike, the woman, the flowers, the sheets . . . this guy probably carried it all in one trip."

"Ya think?" Shelly said.

"I don't see him going back and forth to his car or truck. I guess he parked at least a block away and probably in a real shitty car. He had to make certain it was still there when he came back to it. Anything nice would have been too risky to leave."

"Tom?" Shelly said. "How about a bike?"

"What?" Tom asked.

"Wait a minute Tom, it's possible," Dan said. "My son David had a paper route, Sunday papers. He carried one hundred and twenty pounds on his bike. A big Schwinn, with three baskets."

"Yeah, I've seen bikes like that. It's possible. He could have just peddled right into the house."

Tom agreed. "Hey! Sammy! Shelly, you remember, Sammy. He was always riding his bike around looking for cans," Tom said.

"Right," Shelly said. "He carried nine or ten, full black trash bags. His bike was a corporation. Sammy's bike could carry all that."

"How old was your boy when he had that route, Dan?" Tom asked.

"Fourteen and about one thirty-five soaking wet."

"Big and strong is looking weak," Tom yawned. "Thanks gang, I'll get back to you. I'm beat."

"Sounds good to me, Tom. Shelly are you happy?" Dan asked.

"Who's happy? Tired, yes."

"Anything remarkable in the photos?" Tom asked.

"It's so 'sterile' if you ignore the blood and the mutilation", Shelly said.

"That's it! God you're good Shelly. I've been staring at the pictures for an hour trying to find the right handle. Before the blood and mutilation, white sheets, flowers, clean bike, no dirt in that portion of the room at all. 'Sterile'— that's the word."

"Let's clean up this mess and call it a night. I'm on the carpet in the morning," Tom said.

Shelly passed her pad to Tom. "Good luck, champ."

"Jesus, Shelly," Tom froze as he reached for her pad. "I just realized this is the last time you'll ever do 'Know' 'Don't know' with me. This is your last case, too?"

"That's right, Tom. This is my last case."

"Goodnight, Boys, I'm gone."

Tom watched Shelly leave. "Shelly, may I call you tomorrow night?"

"I'd like that. Goodnight, again."

"Tom, there goes a great lady. If things work out for you two, spend your free time with her. Try and be interested in the things she likes to do."

"Regrets, Dan?" Tom said.

"Some," Dan answered.

"If we get that far, I'll remember what you said. I've got enough regrets."

"Goodnight, Tom."

Tom got out of the car to leave.

"Tom, stop by my house Thursday night. I'll have the title signed. You can use my tags until you get to motor vehicle."

"Thanks, Dan."

Chapter Five

It was just turning midnight. The moon was full and he was happy. It had been a long time since he felt he had accomplished anything worthwhile.

Winning the hundred grand in the Jersey Cash 5 Lottery last year couldn't be considered an accomplishment. It was just dumb luck. If those friggin' losers at the meetings knew, he'd have to hear sob stories and bullshit from all of them.

Boy, oh boy, those drunks could really sniff out a dollar. He liked going to the AA meetings. It was a gas. Everybody is so very serious about his sorry, meaningless life. Just because he was sober ten years, people at the meetings thought he was some sort of damn guru. It was great. Sit there quietly in the back and nod approval when some sick idiot puked out his entire life story. Give him a big hand, afterwards. Tell him how great he was doing. Oh, yeah, and keep coming back. Please, keep coming back, you asshole. I love to hear your bullshit.

His special talent was instigating shit between a couple of these idiots, which wasn't too hard to do. He could get these guys ready to kill each other and the whole time, look like some kind of benevolent gent to them and anyone else around. It was more fun than watching Seinfeld.

"Boy, I really fixed that bitch. She was no damn good." He knew he had done God's will. God told him what to do. He was glad he had joined AA. Prayer never crossed his mind when he was drinking. When it was recommended that he pray, at his first meeting, he was so shook from the booze that he figured, why not. They told him, if he prayed, he might get answers.

He prayed to God. God answered him. He knew God only answered special people. He always knew he was better than everybody. That's why God answered him right away. He told him what to do. Some people made God mad. He figured God used special people, like him, to get even with those who did not do God's will. AA was all about God's will. God sent him to AA to find these people. He told him which people couldn't be saved. Nothing is ever, really, forgiven. He knew that. God wanted them to think they were forgiven, then they would admit their sins at the meetings. Then, he would tell God what they said, and God would tell him how to handle the situation.

God had a good sense of humor. He thought that he probably looked like God.

He was so happy tonight; he wanted to click his heels. His cab looked good, too. He had the best cab around. Michelin tires! No other cab had Michelin tires. Clean windows all the time. Air fresheners! Good air conditioning. He loved driving cab, even more than bullshit. He loved to hear their bullshit. Everyone lied all the time. He knew this. Some steady fares would tell him that they worked here or there at some fancy job. If it were true, why would they tell him? He knew they were lying. He loved to hear their lies. Liars liked to talk. Honest people, who did not lie, were the quiet people. The ones who got in his cab and just gave the address and asked how much, they were not liars. Liars couldn't shut up.

He was quiet. He didn't lie.

He looked at his watch. Twelve fifteen Sunday night, heck, Monday morning, really. That no good bitch got her just desserts, he was happy. God was happy. That's all that mattered.

There were no other cabs this time of the morning. He thought he might have a lot of fun when the next train came in. It was coming; he could hear the whine of it. He knew just how far away it was by the sound. Time to get in the car. He always parked so he could see the departing passengers in his rear view mirror. He liked to see them need his cab. Sometimes, he'd wait and let them catch his cab. But since he was the only cab at the station this morning, he'd have fun. He felt terrific.

"Oh yeah, oh yeah." This guy was in a hurry. Only four people got off the train, tonight. Two young stoners, he knew them. Some old fat lady, and a suit. The suit was running across the platform. Man, he wanted this cab bad. This was great. He really wanted it. He listened to the solid shoes of the suit start to come down the stairs. Oh, boy! He was really moving. What an athlete, a friggin' Bruce Jenner. Well, Brucey old boy, no gold medal for you. Run, Brucey, run! It's your cab, baby! Come on, you can make it!

The suit hit the sidewalk. He thought he should really start timing these guys. He liked to time things; things should be timed.

The suit was behind the cab now. No need to run. No one else looking for a cab. Brucey Baby was first. He'd looked in the rear view mirror hoping to make eye contact with the suit. Come on! Look up! Look at me, you asshole. Yes! Eye contact for just a split second, but contact is contact.

He flips his on-duty light on. Now the suit is jogging. He starts his motor. Here we go! Bruce Jenner is picking up speed, but so is the cab. He yells, but oh no, my radio is too loud. I can't hear you. Oh, he is good. Fifty feet from the back of the cab, now forty, oh, look at him go. Bye, bye, Brucey! I pick up speed. He's still running and waving one arm, now two arms. That's too bad, I guess the cab didn't see you.

The stop sign is ahead. How bad does he want it? Kill the on-duty light. Turn on the inside light, idle and breakout the map.

Come on, Brucey. Maybe I saw you. He's not coming. Oh, yes he is, like a greyhound.

This guy is great. I've got to set up the camera in the trunk. I need film for assholes like this.

The cab waits. Cab waiting. Fifty yards, forty yards, thirty yards, you're going to make it this time. Oh, too bad. Duty light on, interior light out, quick right turn under the tracks and Brucey is gone.

What was that Brucey? I'll tell your mom to wash your mouth out with soap. What a great day!

Chapter Six

Dwayne was an early riser, full of fire in the morning. His routine was to run from five to six. He'd do the run around Cooper River, the section between Route 130 and Cuthbert Boulevard. It was a good run, probably two or three miles. He didn't know exactly how long it was.

He saw a lot of beauty in Camden. It was easy for him. He grew up in Mississippi. He knew Tom thought Camden was a dump, but Tom had never been to Mississippi.

Dwayne wasn't going to run this morning. It was a nice day, a strong breeze out of the Northwest; the air was snappy and fresh. Cool for this time of year, the newscaster said. The high would only be sixty-eight today. Dwayne was excited. He stood on the balcony of his condominium. He had a great view of Philadelphia. He saluted Billy Penn on top of City Hall, with his cup of coffee. "Good morning, Sir," he said. Dwayne loved the cool weather. He could really dress in his best clothes. No jacket and cotton slacks, today. The new three piece he'd been chaffing at the bit to wear would be just right. The day was perfect.

"Close that door, I'm freezing."

He turned to look at his wife. She was hugging herself for warmth. Dwayne laughed, stepped inside, and closed the door. Doris was from Miami and anything below 72 degrees was unacceptable to her.

Gosh, Dwayne thought, how can a woman be that good looking just after rolling out of the sack?

"I'll turn the heat on baby, I didn't think you'd be getting up yet," Dwayne drawled.

"I would have liked to stay in bed. You froze me out," Doris joked. "My father told me not to marry anyone from up North."

"Up North? You mean Mississippi is up North?" Dwayne laughed.

"North of Jacksonville is up North to my daddy."

Dwayne was a morning person and so was Doris. They were a match made in heaven and Dwayne was proud of the choice he had made. His brothers had been married a couple of times; they had made bad choices. Child support payments had them both reduced to paupers. This wouldn't happen to Dwayne. Doris and he were like teenagers on their second date. They were deeply in love.

"Is Tom stopping by this morning, handsome?" she asked as she sat on the sofa.

"Yes, he is," Dwayne said, from the kitchen as he brought her orange juice.

"Florida or California? You know I don't do California?" Doris questioned.

"How can you tell it's not Florida?" Dwayne asked. But he knew, she could tell. He'd tried slipping her California orange juice before, but she wouldn't have it.

"Florida tastes more orange."

Doris never asked what Dwayne was working on. She didn't want to know.

Dwayne didn't feel the need to tell her. She was sweet and spoiled and he liked that about her. Her father was a real estate agent in Miami. Very successful, and Doris was like some sort of princess to him. He liked Dwayne because he knew how to treat Doris. He spoiled her rotten and she loved it. Her daddy loved it, too.

"When does Daddy arrive?" Dwayne asked.

"Flight 204 at 11 a.m. and I hope it's on time. Good Lord, if that flight is late the security people will probably bring him off the plane. He is a handful."

"Whose hands, King Kong's?" Dwayne laughed.

"That's not nice, Dwayne," she laughed, too.

"Well, if you get to the terminal early, you should be able to tell what side of the plane he's sitting on."

"Dwayne!" she warned.

"Baby, it will be leaning to one side." Dwayne buzzed over to her like an airplane in a sharp left-hand turn. Then, fell next to her on the sofa.

Doris laughed in spite of herself. She could imagine the plane listing. Daddy wasn't called "Big Daddy" for nothing. He weighed about four hundred pounds.

"Dwayne, you're mean."

"Honey, you know I love Daddy."

"I know you do, now give me some sugar."

The doorbell rang. The building has a buzzer at the mailboxes in the foyer, but after six in the morning, the doorman lets the doors open to air the lobby. He'd watch who came in, but if they looked okay, he'd just smile and say, "Good morning." People liked this. It gave the high rise a neighborly feeling.

Doris said, "Honey, get off me! I've got to get dressed!"

"Tom will wait. He can probably guess what two young, beautiful people are doing."

"Stop it, Dwayne, that would embarrass me. I don't want anyone guessing something like that." She ran for the bedroom.

Dwayne laughed. She was so sweet. He liked this about her, too. She was tall, beautiful and classy. She never dressed sexy. He thought to himself, she isn't *like* a princess, she *is* a princess. She could have given Princess Diana lessons on how to behave, and that Fergie, too.

Dwayne liked to talk aloud to himself. He had a good voice. He smiled as he went to open the door.

"Where's my baby?" a big voice boomed.

"Hey! Big Daddy!" Dwayne and Big Daddy hugged.

Big Daddy hugged, anyway. He was a hugger. Dwayne always felt like a child when Big Daddy hugged him. He would just pray it was a short hug, so he could resume breathing.

Doris flew down the hall. Big Daddy dumped Dwayne in a chair like a sack of potatoes.

"Daddy," she jumped up and he caught her effortlessly. For a big man he was agile and strong. He used to play pro football. Dwayne thought he might have lost a step or two, but no more.

"Dwayne, go outside and help those boys," Big Daddy said as he carried the love of his life across the room.

Dwayne took a deep breath, got up, and looked down the hallway. Two young kids were trying to make it to the door with Daddy's luggage. A white kid and a black kid, both about 10 years old. In the neighborhood, they were both considered to be Dennis the Menace, but everyone liked them, and you could tell they liked each other. As they struggled with the bags, they were busting up laughing. Dwayne couldn't remember seeing them when they weren't laughing. It brought back memories of himself at 10. He hadn't laughed much.

"What's so funny, you two?" Dwayne asked. These kids were infectuously funny, they always made him laugh.

Ernest tried to speak, but it wasn't possible. He just looked at Dwayne and doubled up in laughter. "Steve . . . Stevie's got shrimps in his ass." More outrageous laughter. Ernest had to set his bags down. He was out of control.

"I do not," Steve yelled. "They're down my pants, not in my ass." Steve tried in vain to keep a straight face as he spoke, but one look at Ernest and he lost it.

Dwayne looked at the boys, and he lost his composure. He had to wedge himself between the frame of the door, to stop from falling over laughing.

Daddy and Doris were walking to the door. They looked at Dwayne and now they started to laugh. Doris put her hand on Dwayne's arm as he shook with laughter. They looked down the hallway. "What's happening, Dwayne?" Doris chuckled.

"Ernest says Stevie has shrimps in his ass," Dwayne whispered to them. Stevie was struggling with a case of shrimp. Some shrimp were falling out and he was definitely squirming.

Big Daddy roared with laughter. It seemed like the walls shook. Doris had to head for the sofa, holding her stomach. Everyone fell apart in laughter.

The busybody across the hall opened his door. "This is a fine way to be awakened," he announced.

He really was a screamer. I mean you could tell he was gay a mile away. Big Daddy took one look at his Wizard of Oz bathrobe and his shaved legs and he lost it. He looked at Dwayne, Dwayne looked at Big Daddy, and that was it. They were gone now. The combination of the happy and unexpected arrival, Stevie's shrimp problems, Ernest laying on the floor doubled up in laughter, kicking his feet so he wouldn't wet himself was just too much for Dwayne. He pushed Daddy back inside and they closed the door. The condo was bedlam.

Daddy was crying in laughter, holding on to Doris. Dwayne opened the door to tell the boys to come on in, but Monte was still at his door, with his hand on his hip. He reminded Dwayne of a disapproving teacher he had as a kid. Dwayne started laughing all over again. Daddy was getting it together, until he got a second gander at Monte. Then it started again. Falling against Doris and howling in laughter, Dwayne shut the door with his foot and fell into a chair.

It took about five minutes for them to get back to normal. They were almost cooled down, when Big Daddy said, "Shrimps." That was it. They fell apart one more time. Doris ran for the bathroom while Big Daddy yelled, "Don't be in there long."

Dwayne was doubled up in the chair, his stomach hurt.

Big Daddy said, "I'll get the door for the boys, but if Judy Garland's still across the hall, you better call an ambulance for me."

Dwayne pulled himself together and grabbed a tissue to wipe his eyes. He passed one to Daddy.

Daddy opened the door slowly. Thank God, Monte was gone. The kids had made it to the door. Daddy, stilled chuckling, waved them in. He took the bags from Ernest, and peeled two twenties from a big roll. "Here boys, I've paid a lot more for a lot less fun."

The boys smiled. Stevie was blushing. Dwayne watched them rush toward the elevator shouting, "Thanks a lot, Mister," still laughing.

Dwayne closed the door. He walked back into the living room with Daddy and Doris. They were happy to be together, the three of them.

Chapter Seven

The bell rang. Dwayne knew it was Tom. He guessed he had done all the laughing that he would do for today. He answered on the speakerphone and told Tom he would be right down.

Tom asked Dwayne to drive. He was not a morning person. Grouchy, and not very talkative until he had had his coffee.

"Coffee?" Dwayne asked.

Tom nodded, put his head back, and closed his eyes. He wasn't thinking, yet. Just resting his eyes. They pulled into the parking lot of the White Lantern. Alice had his coffee waiting. He'd feel better soon. Coffee with cream, no sugar. That was his kicker in the morning.

Only water, for Dwayne, an early riser. He'd had his coffee. "I had some trouble last night," Dwayne said.

"Let me guess. You couldn't get the warrant."

"Right the first time," Dwayne replied.

"Was any explanation given?"

"They told me I would know 'why' tomorrow."

"Tomorrow is today. We're off to see the Mayor," Tom said dryly.

"What's up? Any ideas?" Dwayne asked.

Tom grunted. The coffee hadn't kicked in, yet.

Dwayne and Tom left the Lantern. Dwayne drove and thought of Big Daddy. Doris was probably unwrapping some gift she didn't need and had to have. Big Daddy was probably looking around the condo to make sure everything was top shelf. Heck, the last time he was up, he'd had a new dishwasher installed. Said the old one was too noisy. Dwayne remembered the boys in the hallway. 'Boys in the hall', where had he heard that before?

Anyway, those boys were a riot. He thought maybe he'd ask their folks if he could take them to a ball game. Doris and he had been going to the fertility clinic to find out where his 'little slugger' was.

"It's gotta be Feds."

"What?" Dwayne was sorry he said it already. He was determined not to keep sticking his foot in the same trap.

Tom gave him the 'stupid' look, but only for a split second. "The warrant. It's the only way it figures," Tom said.

"Remember the Feds raiding the Sanchez Brothers in North Camden a couple of months ago?"

"Yes, but where's the tie in?" Dwayne said.

"One of my snitches dimed Mag at the Sanchez place a couple of times that week."

"Mag, out in the open, with those creeps?" Dwayne drawled.

"That's right, I smell rat."

They drove into the Court House Complex. The Mayor's car was there, so was a brand new Ford. They headed up the steps toward the lobby. The building was imposing, all white stone. They can't build them like this anymore, Tom thought. It would cost a fortune. Though stately and beautiful on the outside, the interior rooms had long ago been sectioned off for one purpose or another. It was a rabbit warren.

The Mayor's office was on the second floor. Tom pointed to a narrow set of stairs. Dwayne was glad. He knew the elevator was used for everything from taking bodies to the lab, to running food up to the prisoners on the fifth floor. It usually had some awful smell and it wasn't wise to lean on the walls. You could get stuck.

They walked past a lady on a bench, who was crying. She could have been crying for a million different reasons. A lot of crying was done here. Not much smiling. Well, Court Houses weren't comedy clubs. Although some poor defendants thought their Public Defenders were comedians. They continued on to the office of the Mayor and were greeted by a secretary who said, "Name and business, please."

"Lieutenant Tom White and Sergeant Dwayne Cherry. We have an appointment with Her Honor."

"That's right, I have it right here." The secretary looked like she came with the building, around the turn of the century. She didn't miss a beat, though.

"Mayor, White and Cherry are here," she said, speaking into an intercom.

"Go right in gentlemen. She's waiting."

"Thank you," Tom said.

Dwayne nodded and smiled. She didn't smile back. She was efficient. A smile wasn't necessary and at her age, moving that face was probably real work.

They walked the short distance to an old oak door, knocked and were told to enter.

"Hello, Tom, it's good to see you."

"Hello, Ann, this is Dwayne Cherry."

"Hello, Dwayne, I've only heard good things about you from the District Attorney." Mayor Ann Robinson said all this through the phoniest smile in the state.

Tom had been here before. He couldn't stand her. She spoke barely moving her mouth. Maybe she was afraid her teeth would fall out, couldn't be. They were too large to be dentures, horse teeth. Tom thought she looked like her secretary. The secretary had to be the Mayor's Mom.

"Tom, I'm busy and this is going to be a short meeting. Don't balk at what this Agent has to say. There are people who know the reasons for what he's going to tell you. It's all strictly on a need to know basis."

Tom knew what was coming. He was no virgin.

"This is Agent Smith, Alcohol, Tobacco and Firearms. Agent Smith, the floor is yours," said the Mayor.

He launched right into it. "Sorry to tell you this, but our Agency has known about Mag's mother's place for months. I can tell you, Mag is working for us on a case we've been developing for a little over a year. A lot of money and time has been used to get to the point where we are."

"The long and short," Tom said.

"Leave Mag alone. In two weeks he'll be in protective custody and we expect him to testify against many large players."

Tom wondered if this kid shaved yet. He didn't think so. He said, "That's fine, but what about his stash?"

"Stay away from the house. We know every aspect of his operation. Leave the stash in the house and don't go near it. I hope you understand."

"It rubs me the wrong way," Tom said, "but I was in the service before I joined the force. I understand how things have to be sometimes. Thank you for your time Agent Smith and Mayor Robinson. I know how busy you are."

Tom continued, "As a matter of fact, there's a fresh murder case that's got me baffled. I wonder, Mayor, if I could select a few men, just two, other than

Officer Cherry, and form a task force to get it cleaned up. Two or three weeks would do it, I think, if we could work on it, exclusively. I know it's a lot to ask, but this is a case that cries for results."

"I like the cut of your jib, Lieutenant," Agent Smith said.

Where do the Feds get these corny kids, Tom wondered.

Agent Smith looked at the Mayor. The Mayor didn't even blink.

"Tom, I like your sense of duty. You'd make a good Captain. I'll arrange your task force and I hope you get your murderer," she smiled.

"Right now, I'm just scratching my head, but I think the four of us will be able to clean it up. I *will* need jurisdiction over everyone in the Department at the murder scene. It's only one block, both sides of the street. You know how the Captain can queer things, throwing his weight around. I'm certain the killer will return, if we're discreet."

Mayor Robinson answered, "I know too well, about the Captain, Tom. Good luck. I'll tell the Captain you want one block to yourself for three weeks. If he interferes with you, I'll have his badge. I'll tell him at lunch. Call him this evening and tell him where your murder scene is. He'll stay away."

"Thanks, Mayor. Goodbye, Agent Smith." Tom shook hands vigorously with the agent and almost bowed to the Mayor on the way out of the office. Dwayne followed Tom.

Tom walked out fast, Dwayne followed closely and he could see Tom's ears starting to turn red. In the lobby Tom stopped at a fountain, wet a handkerchief and held it first to one ear and then the other.

"I guess you're wondering why I'm wetting my ears. It's simple. That old witch up there knows when I'm angry my ears turn red. Hell! It's a company joke."

Dwayne said, "When I knew I'd be your temporary partner, only about two dozen cops told me to watch out if they got red."

"I'll bet they did. When we walk past her window, in thirty seconds, they're not going to be red. She's up there right now, looking out the window for that red flag. If she sees it, she'll know I was running some game. How do they look?"

"Left one is normal. Put a little more water on the right one."

"She won't see the right one. Let's go." Tom walked out and stood by the car, casually lighting a cigarette. They got into the car.

"Is she at the window? Tell me when we go by."

"She's there, just now turning around," Dwayne said.

"What struck you as odd about that little farce up there?" Tom asked.

"The District Attorney wasn't there or the Captain."

"That's right, and they always brown nose the Feds," said Tom.

"Do you think the Fed was alone?" Dwayne asked.

"Oh, I doubt it, they come in two's. We probably just made a damn film, or at least, a recording."

"What's really up?" Dwayne asked.

"I don't know, but something's not right."

"Well, you sure got us out of a lot of work. One case, for three weeks. That's sweet," Dwayne said.

"Think," Tom said, "What's on that block besides the murder scene?"

"Oh, shit, Tom."

"That's right."

"Why do I feel like I just lost the job in the District Attorney's office," Dwayne groaned.

"If this is what I think it is, you might be the next D.A."

Dwayne's eyes popped. "What do you mean?" he said.

"Not now. Let's get Willis and Ready," Tom said.

"Willis and Ready?" Dwayne asked.

"That's right. The odd couple," Tom said.

"Tom! I feel sick."

"Then you've got good instincts, so do I."

Chapter Eight

Tom drove down Broadway past the stores that sold beepers, crummy sports clothing, and expensive sneakers. The pimps were out, although it was only a little after nine in the morning. It was the end of a long shift for them. They had to work the bus station, though. They looked good when they were at the station, not too flashy. Most of them showed just enough jewelry to let any young runaway know that they had money. The unfortunate girls that ended up in Camden broke and homeless wouldn't go hungry if the pimps could help it.

A pimp could spot a girl in trouble in one fifth of a second. The victim would be looking tired, lost and confused. It was so easy for them; it made Tom sick. More than once he'd watched a pimp walk out of the terminal with a girl, so fresh from the farm, so beautiful, he would have cut off a finger to have a date with her. What shocked Tom was how fast it happened. Oh, they had a million different lines for the girls. Like a Mercedes mechanic, they knew precisely which tool to use for each girl. Drugs, if the girl looked strung out. Conversation, for the lonely types. Job offers, for the stupid. A different approach was used on each victim. They didn't score that often, but they didn't have to; one girl a month was all the pimp needed to make a great living.

A reformed pimp told Tom, that he had gone to the bus terminal for three years, every morning. Over the period of one month, he would hit on ninety to a hundred girls. Eventually, he would get his lady. The pimp told him it was usually a girl that was ready to give up on life. When you look at numbers like a hundred a month, you realized that the pimp couldn't fail. The pimp told him, first, you take her to get something to eat. Then, you take her to a motel, give her the key, leave her some food, smokes and anything else she wants. You let her rest. A day later, after she thinks she's been alone long enough, she's usually watched, you stroll back to the motel. You take her shopping, to dinner and a movie. Then, he'd make love to her. Tell her how much she mattered to him. He'd get her to talk. That was the most important part. Once he knew her head, she was his.

Some of the girls were tough, though. Some started screaming and didn't want to make love, he'd just let them go, but after years of practice in the selection of these girls, based on a fifteen second evaluation at the terminal, he batted about five hundred. He usually got them working on the street in less than a week. With one girl on the street, fresh and new, he'd reap three grand a week. Six months later, no one wanted her. Six months on the streets here and a young girl was old.

Dwayne sat next to Tom as they drove south on Broadway. He was no fool. Whatever Tom had in mind, if it looked like he was crossing the line, he could cross it without Dwayne. He'd go back to the Mayor if he had to. Damn it! Tom was at the end of his career and he knew Tom knew it. The Mayor knew it. No way did the Mayor think Tom would make a good Captain. She was blowing smoke up his ass. Dwayne was pissed at this whole thing. Dwayne thought the Mayor probably didn't know a whole lot about Tom, aside from the red ear problem. But that was a standing joke. She hadn't been the Mayor long enough to know how Tom worked. Her ear to the men was through the Captain. Dwayne knew the Captain spent most of his time with her blowing his own horn. The Captain was a selfish man. He'd screwed just about every cop on the force, one time or another. Everyone knew he got Captain after thirty years of stepping on people. First, his partners, then squads, next divisions, now the whole damn force. If he ever became Mayor, he'd step on the whole city.

Dwayne exhaled. It was a beautiful day. He felt great in his new suit. He was glad he had worn it. He must have looked good in the Mayor's office. He chuckled to himself.

"Damn," he laughed, "I am a brown-noser."

He looked out the window and smiled at the city, brown-nosers make it here. That's why Tom would be a lieutenant when he retired. Tom couldn't brown-nose.

"Oh no, nobody's getting me in trouble."

Dwayne knew why he thought this way. Up and Out. That's what he used to say in Mississippi. He remembered what good luck he had as a boy down home. He worked for some white folks as a lad. He did their yard work, washed their cars, their dogs and whatever else they wanted done, he had done with a smile. Some white folks liked him. Some thought he was just an eager Uncle Tom. He didn't give a darn what they thought. It kept him away from home and his father, and that was enough.

Dwayne's mother had disappeared when he was a child, after she had received a severe beating at the hands of his father. He felt pretty sure that his father had killed her. Lots of other people who knew his old man thought it was likely. The Sheriff had talked to his old man about it. Dwayne remembered that Sheriff. He had pulled up in front of the house one evening, if you could call two rooms with a cold-water tap, a house. The Sheriff waved his father over to the car and asked him where Renee was. The old man had said that she'd run off. The Sheriff didn't even get out of the car. That was good enough for him, it was Mississippi.

Dwayne wondered to himself about whether it was luck or fate that changed his life. He was fifteen years old and had been working for Judge Beecham the day his big break had come. The Judge's only son had been riding his dirt bike all afternoon. The brat had already buzzed Dwayne a few times. Dwayne was planting ivy along the long driveway leading to their beautiful, stately home. The old house had been spared the ravages of the Civil War. It still looked like a slave plantation, and the Judge still worked his help like slaves.

Dwayne could hear the Judge chuckle every time his son buzzed Dwayne. He thought the sun rose and set on his Timothy. At one end of the drive was a small paddock. The Judge's prize bull was kept there. That bull was for stud, and it was in demand. The Judge loved it. He liked to watch it at its work. He'd laugh, "That ain't love, but it sure is money." The Judge had a thousand sayings, but only he could see the humor in most of them.

This afternoon the boy buzzed Dwayne a little too closely. The peg of his bike struck a pallet of ivy. The bike was sliding down the drive, the boy right behind. Both boy and bike slid under the bottom bar of the pipe fence, into the paddock. The Judge's bull, General Hooker, wheeled away from his drinking water. This bull was mean. His name, General Hooker, was given to him after hooking, goring and killing a cow that didn't take to his advances. The Judge paid for the cow, but wouldn't have the massive horns trimmed. He had enjoyed the killing. He watched, from his front porch, while the bull worked his awful horns, hooking the carcass, this way and that. He enjoyed the kill.

"Look how he hooks. I'm naming him 'General Hooker', it suits him."

But this day, as boy and bike slid into the paddock, the bull wheeled and stood. Dwayne wasn't the only one Timmy had buzzed that day. Timmy had teased the bull, also.

General Hooker was about fifty yards from the unconscious boy. Dwayne was about fifty feet away. As the dust was settling, he heard the Judge scream. It was a scream from deep within. Dwayne was shocked; not by the accident, or the scream, but from suddenly realizing the Judge had real feelings, deep feelings. His love for his boy was in that scream.

Dwayne walked slowly toward the paddock. The bull was pawing, but he hadn't moved yet. Dwayne prayed he wouldn't move.

The Judge yelled to Dwayne, "That's right boy, don't spook him. Please, Dwayne, get my son out of there."

Dwayne thought to himself, "All the Judge's money, all the politicians that he knew, even the people who owed him favors, couldn't help him at this instant. Right now, Dwayne Cherry was the only person in the world that the Judge needed.

Dwayne was shocked. He would have bet the Judge thought his name was 'boy' and he'd never heard the Judge say 'please' to anyone.

Timmy groaned and rolled over on his back, semi-conscious. His motion aroused the bull and he charged. Dwayne flew to the paddock, dove through the first and second rail. Timmy was right there; Dwayne thought he could make it. He didn't look at anything but Timmy. He had to get Timmy out. Dwayne picked him up, turned to the fence and threw him over. Then, he felt the pain.

The bull had hooked him through the thigh. Dwayne saw the sky, then the ground, then the sky. He felt the hot dry ground as he landed on his back, outside of the paddock. He saw the sky go black. As he was passing out, he smiled.

Dwayne awoke in a beautiful room. It was morning. He could hear the doves. The Judge was in a chair next to the bed.

Dwayne raised his head an inch and asked, "How's Timmy?"

The Judge looked up. "Thank you, God." He started to cry. Through his tears, he said, "Timmy's just scratched up. He'll be okay."

"That's good," Dwayne said.

"Listen son," the Judge said, "You broke a few bones, but you're going to be okay. I have called your father and asked him to let you live here with me, if that's okay with you."

Dwayne's head swirled. "Do you mean here on the farm?"

"Hell no. Here, in this house. Three days ago I almost lost my son, now I have two sons, and believe me Dwayne, when I say that. Dwayne, I'm going to treat you like a son, and you'll have everything that goes with that."

"What will people say, me being here?" Dwayne asked.

"I don't care what anyone says. If that bull had gotten to Timmy, it would have finished me. I couldn't go on after that."

The Judge had been true to his word. 'Everything that went with it,' is just what he got. He lived in the main house for the next three years and finished his high school. He was sent to the University of Tennessee and he hadn't looked back since. Yeah, was it luck or fate? He still wondered.

Dwayne noticed that they were almost out of the city.

"Tom, where are we going?"

Tom didn't reply.

Dwayne leaned back, waiting for his answer. He wouldn't step in the trap.

Ten minutes later, Tom said, "We're going to Gloucester."

"Okay," Dwayne smiled, "Just wondered."

Dwayne and Tom got out of the car at the park just off King Street in Gloucester City. Gloucester was just south of Camden. Tom liked to come here to stroll and think. Stand and think, anyway. It wasn't large enough for a stroll, but the river was here and Tom could let his mind formulate battle plans. He didn't force himself to come up with any solutions. The river rolling out to the Delaware Bay and the sea would bring them to him.

"Tom, what did you mean, 'I might be the next D.A.',," Dwayne asked.

"I was just steamed."

"No, come on, you think the D.A.'s dirty?" asked Dwayne.

Tom answered, "Dwayne, I wish they were all dirty. The Mayor, the Captain, the D.A., that would make things easier."

"What then?"

"I don't think they're dirty, just stone stupid and criminally inept."

Dwayne snickered, "Well, they are city employees. It goes with the territory, doesn't it?"

"Damn it, Dwayne! We're city employees."

"No we're not. We're cops, we work for the people."

"Yeah, I forgot, 'To serve and protect', thanks for reminding me. You know Dwayne, you're cheering me up.

"So why the red ears?" Dwayne smiled.

Tom smiled too, and leaned on the rail, listening to the traffic overhead on the Walt Whitman Bridge. He lit up a smoke.

"Dwayne, the Federal boys have somebody, somewhere, that they're hot to burn."

"So?" Dwayne asked.

"Just relax and let me talk, okay?"

"Okay, don't get red."

"So they come to town and find slime like Mag. How they get to him doesn't really matter, but they do. He's probably the largest street distributor in the City of Camden. Probably feeding twenty or thirty corners. With I'd guess, a hundred punks dealing for him. For two years we've been on roofs, in basements, sitting in shitty vans, trying to find his stash. We find it. We can't touch it. Meanwhile, Mag's poison keeps on moving to the corners. Maybe I'm the stupid one, but I really believe that the couple of kids that overdose on that shit are more important than some sixty year old scumbag in Cuba, Panama, Columbia or wherever the hell else this guy is that the Feds are trying to capture. I say, 'Fuck Panama.' I'm worried about Americans in Camden, and I don't like being told to spend a few souls, especially by some Federal hick in a dark suit."

"So what do we do now?" Dwayne questioned.

"Off the top of my head, you take Maria Antoinette Gonzales to the friggin' movies and I firebomb the house."

"You're joking!" Dwayne hoped.

"I'm not joking, but I'm not serious, either," Tom said.

"We've got to go along, Tom. Like you said, we probably just made a film. They'd throw us under Marion Prison if we messed up their investigation."

"Relax! Don't get scared. I can just hear the guys at the Donut Shop telling you I'll get your ass in a sling."

"It's happened, hasn't it?" Dwayne asked.

"Yeah, but not lately. I'm smarter now," winked Tom.

"Tom, I've got a wife. Can I relax? No crazy moves?"

Tom laughed, "Take a chill pill, will ya?"

"I'm chilling, Tom."

"Good, Nervous Nellie."

"So, the D.A. thing?" Dwayne asked.

"You'll go far Dwayne, you don't give up. What I meant by that was if someone went public that we (meaning the Mayor and the Feds) are letting the largest dope dealer in the city operate, I think there would be a big shake up at the polls."

"But the Feds?" Dwayne asked.

"People don't give a shit about the Feds. They care about their children and their neighbors' children." Tom's ears were really red now.

"Would someone have to go public?"

"Dwayne! You crafty son-of-a-bitch."

"I guess a tip would come back to us, huh?" Dwayne said.

"It would, if the tip-off came today," said Tom.

"Next week?" Dwayne asked.

"If the Mayor tells the Captain about the Feds today at lunch, I think next week might work. We'll keep our ears open. If we hear the same skinny from another source, then it's a whole new ball game."

"What's the risk factor for us?" Dwayne asked.

"They might questions us, but a week from now, hell, they couldn't be sure."

Dwayne had a worried look on his face and said, "I know I suggested the tip, but don't think I'd call it in. Now, or a month from now. I was just thinking out loud, Tom."

"You'll go far, Dwayne."

"Damn right, Lieutenant."

"I wonder how Jesus and Rosa made out last night. Shit, what really pisses me off is the fact that we had that stash."

Tom said, "Lighten up, I've got to think the Feds would have given it back to Mag. Sickening, isn't it?"

"Absolutely."

"Dwayne, you know when I realized this country was truly a nut house?"

"No."

"When they let the guy who murdered nineteen people testify and then they turned him lose in our great country."

"That made a lot of people sick," said Dwayne.

"How'd you feel about it?" Tom asked.

"I didn't really think too much about it, Tom."

"You'll go far, Dwayne."

"Is that a crack, Tom?"

"No, just my way of saying you'll do well in the D.A.'s office. They've got deals there, too."

"Oh."

"Forget it! We're going to get together tomorrow at the White Lantern, eight a.m."

"And today?" Dwayne asked.

"I'm going to investigate at the Shore."

"How's that work?" Dwayne asked.

"I'm going to throw a hook in the ocean and see if I can pull out any evidence. You never know."

"And if a fluke gets in the way?"

"Fluke are careless like that," Tom said.

"Okay, what do you want me to do today, Tom?"

"I want you to get in touch with the Odd Couple. Tell them about our meeting tomorrow at eight a.m. at the Lantern, no excuses, be there."

"Tom, did those two ever work together on a case?" Dwayne asked.

"Yeah! It gets pretty ugly, but it works," Tom answered.

"But Tom, Ready's a damn racist, isn't he?"

"Yeah, but so is Willis. It evens out."

"But Willis likes you, he told me."

Tom laughed, "Every racist has an exception or two, I'm his."

"Does Ready have any exceptions?" Dwayne asked.

"I don't know, Dwayne, but if you're real nice, maybe you'll be his first."

"Oh, this is gonna be great. And after I do that, what do you want me to do?"

"Take the day off. Doris's Dad's up. Have some fun," said Tom.

"Let's get out of here, then," Dwayne said.

"We're going! I'll drive you home."

"I hope Doris doesn't have Daddy at the mall, yet."

Changing the subject abruptly, Tom said, "I'll call Dan Gross this afternoon to see if he has anything else for us.

"Tom, we haven't even talked about the murder case today."

"I can't. I was up all night thinking about it. I didn't shut an eye until four a.m. If you don't back off sometime, you'll swallow your gun."

"I've been a cop long enough to know that. But, thanks for the day off. Doris likes having Big Daddy and Dwayne with her. It means a lot to her to spend time with both of us, together."

"There you go, Dwayne. Just when I'm certain that you're a selfish creep, you spoil it," Tom smiled.

"Tom, Ready bringing that dog with him?"

Tom laughed heartily as Dwayne exited the car.

Chapter Nine

As he rowed out into the river, he laughed to himself. This is so sweet. Ten years ago, if someone had told him he would be a sponsor for some sick alcoholic, who wanted to spill his whole life story to him, he would have said they were crazy. But ten years ago, no one even spoke to him. People ignored homeless drunks.

Tonight was special. Fourth Step, what a kick in the ass. Marco was going to spill the beans to him, of all people. If Marco lied, he would be able to tell. If he told the truth, and Marco just might . . . Oh, Mama!

He rowed steadily, but not too fast, with his back to Marco. It was a good thing that they were back to back. Marco was taking this AA forgiveness thing, very seriously. It wouldn't look right to him, if he could see the ear-to-ear grin on his sponsor's face.

Marco was praying. His sponsor had told him to pray for forgiveness. What a dope! That's like praying to be ten feet tall. Forgiveness.

He thought of the bitch. She was his friend. She told him her story. He got her a job, and Diane, to be her sponsor. She could have told the truth. She was quiet when he first met her. They were friends. She started talking more and more between meetings. More lies. She'd had an abortion; she never told me that. She had left that little fact out of her "story". It was a shame she had to die. But, God's will.

He'd had feelings for her. He'd really miss her. She was a great bullshitter.

Most people didn't know the difference between bullshit and lies. Most people didn't know there was a difference. Asshole Jerry from AA says they're the same. Lies and bullshit, night and day, not the same thing at all. But then, Jerry wasn't special. God told him that! But, God must have a place for Jerry, or he wouldn't be thinking about him now, as he rowed Marco out into the channel.

"Amen," said Marco.

Oh, poor Marco! Forgot he was there. Let's see. The channel is right about here. He'd try to turn around with a straight face, but it didn't much matter. A strong light on the stern would silhouette him. He was excited. He could laugh right in Marco's face. He'd be blind.

"This is it, Marco. Time to admit your sins to God."

"If the program says it will help, I'm ready."

He hoped it would be good stuff, but he doubted it. The only reason that he asked God about Marco was because he was so boring at the meetings. One night in the parking lot, after a meeting, he had almost shot him. But God spoke to him and said, "Not now! You're too special to go to jail for that bore." So he had waited for the right time to come around and it had.

"Marco, before you begin your Fourth Step, I'll pray with you." He lowered his head. He was excited. Marco's stupid face was so serious he had to laugh. No! Don't laugh! Wait!

Most of the drunks started talking about their drinking problems from the age of about fifteen. Their story was supposed to start then. He would time Marco. If he started at the age of fifteen, he should make it on time. The beautiful thing about being sober for ten years, was that these idiots trusted you, completely. Fools, if he could drink, he would. But he had hardly any liver left, a couple of drinks and he was sick. He'd followed Marco home and when he was in a blind spot, he pulled up to him.

"Marco, it's time for your Fourth Step," he shouted. "Get in."

He just got in the cab, blind obedience, just because someone can't drink.

No one knows where he is. Now, he's sitting in a rowboat in the middle of a river on a dark night.

How he ever got to be thirty years old is a wonder. Hope he's not boring. God long ago promised him he wouldn't have to suffer a bore.

"Amen! You have the chair, Marco. Go ahead."

"Well, my first experience with alcohol started, when my mother put paregoric on my gums." He had turned to face the rower.

"Excuse me, Marco, if you turn around and face the water, it should be less embarrassing and help you open up. Face to face, you might tend to be inhibited."

"It will help," he said.

He sat in the back of the boat. This guy's out of time. "Paregoric when I was a baby."

The anchor split Marco's head wide open. He stuck his fingers in Marco's skull. Marco's brains ran away from his hard fingers. Now he understood the saying, "Soft in the head." He laid down to laugh. But Marco had been quite a disappointment. Marco never would have been done on time.

"Bye bye, Marco. Over you go, buddy." He hadn't lied to Marco; it had helped him open up. He felt good, but he'd felt better. Bored to death, he laughed. Oh my, now that's funny, bored to death.

Maybe somebody needs a cab.

Chapter Ten

Tom had called the Captain and given him the address of the crime scene. The Captain wasn't aware that Mag's stash was on the same block. Tom didn't think he would be. There weren't any restaurants in that neighborhood. The Captain hadn't paid for a meal in years. He'd always dodge the check. The fat slob was killing himself with a knife and fork. Tom didn't know what spin the Mayor had put on his request, but she was a politician. The Captain didn't seem miffed, just in a hurry. It must have been feeding time.

Tom wasn't going fishing. He was headed to Marlton to see his dentist. He'd put off getting his teeth bleached. It was time. The date with Shelly was getting him nervous. He wasn't good at dating. He thought about the women he had dated. Hindsight showed him that he had only asked them out after they had proffered many, not too subtle hints. He really hadn't gone after them, but they let him think he had. They had all made the first move.

His thoughts returned to the dentist visit. What a racket they had going. As a child his mom would drag him to a dentist on Main Street in Riverton. This dentist had huge hands the size of pie plates. Fingers as thick as sausages. With these handicaps, which they must have been, he had still managed to install four permanent fillings per visit. His present dentist just might, mind you, might fill one tooth with a temporary filling on the third visit. First it was the cleaning, then the ex-rays, then the temporary filling. What a crook he was. Equal to many that he had investigated, he felt. A racket, in his estimation.

Tom pulled into the lot. He had called earlier and asked to speak to the dentist. The secretary was rather balky about putting him on the telephone, until Tom told her he was a lieutenant on the police force and she better get off her ass and get him on the line. He rarely spoke to anyone like that, but she was acting both stupid and rude. He could deal with stupid; it came with the job. He could deal with rude, that was another part of his job. But both stupid and rude in one person was totally unacceptable. He wondered how she kept her job.

He entered the office and took a look at the receptionist. She was cheap looking, but sexy. Really sexy. He'd seen hookers on the job with longer skirts. Her blouse top was totally useless; she could have left it at home for all it covered. He found himself wondering if the dentist's wife had ever been to the office. No way. She was probably way over paid. But, no doubt about it, she'd keep her job.

As Tom left the dentist's office he was wondering when he had started thinking the worst about people. Not the people he knew, just the rest of the world. As it turned out, the dentist might be a crook, but he wasn't married. The cheap looking receptionist was his fiancée and the dentist was really in love with her. The dentist was about forty, not even a little bit above average, a little portly and slightly balding. Tom had to smile to himself. A crystal ball wasn't needed to see the dentist's future. Two years of great sex followed by a really nasty divorce. He thought how different the receptionist would look in divorce court after her lawyer coached her in deportment, dress and makeup. Heck, she'd probably look like a schoolteacher. She'd live in his house with the child and a large monthly check. He'd probably move back in with his mom, and start crying on some barmaid's shoulder. Maybe the barmaid would be number two. Tom wondered why really smart men, like the dentist, picked the wrong women. Of course, he hadn't picked her at all. She had picked him and the next thing to be picked would be his pocket. Justice, he thought. The dentist picked his pocket and the receptionist picks the dentist's pocket.

Tom looked at his teeth in the Jeep's mirror. They did look whiter, not really white yet, but better. His mouth was sore and a bit red but that was to be expected.

Tom started the Jeep and turned back toward the city. As he turned onto the highway, he thought of Dwayne and Ready working together and he smiled. It wasn't right and he knew it, but sometimes Ready was funny. Like any white cop, Tom had heard his share of racial humor. He figured that Dwayne probably got the other side of the coin from Willis. Tom knew that black cops had their little racial jokes, too. Dwayne had spent some considerable time with Willis before he was married. Tom was sure Doris didn't care for

Willis. He could guess why. Willis looked at a woman from the soles of her shoes and slowly worked his eyes upward. He'd seen hookers squirm at one of these examinations. Doris didn't suffer fools gladly, and he was sure she thought him a fool.

He thought of Doris. Before meeting her, he had called Dwayne at home. He would have bet a week's salary he was talking to a white woman. Doris had been to the best schools; Big Daddy had made certain of that. No public schools for his princess. She hadn't even been in a classroom with the opposite sex until she went to college. Dwayne was the first man she ever dated. She met him at Tennessee. Tom laughed now, thinking of Dwayne's story of his first meeting with Big Daddy.

Dwayne had been dating Doris for only one month. He was knocking on her apartment door. They were late for the football game. Dwayne had no idea how close Doris and her father were. Her father opened the door and Dwayne quickly slipped a small package back into his pocket. Tom remembered the conversation as Dwayne had told it.

"So you're Dwayne Cherry. Come in," her father said.

"Hello, is Doris here?"

"Right now, son, you better just concern yourself with what's right in front of you."

"I don't get it," Dwayne blinked. "Where's Doris?"

"She's in the bedroom getting ready for the game. I'm her father."

"Oh, hello. I'm Dwayne Cherry."

"Come on in the kitchen, Dwayne, let's jaw a bit."

Dwayne followed her father down a hallway to a large kitchen. He was surprised by the gentlemen that he saw sitting around the table in that room. The kitchen wasn't large anymore. Big Daddy had three of his former teammates from the Rams with him. They were all five years away from the field, but still impressive and huge. Dwayne thought that the four together had to weigh three-quarters of a ton. The one hundred and sixty pounds he had been flexing in front of his mirror an hour ago, suddenly, seemed frail.

Dwayne wasn't going to show any fear.

"Hi, I'm Dwayne," he said as he offered his hand to the men. They hadn't moved a muscle. They were looking at him like a two-day-old slice of pizza, he said.

"Forget the introductions, son, you might not be here that long." Big Daddy could look plenty mean and that day, he was doing a good job of it. "My daughter thinks a lot of you. I think maybe too much. She's only known you a month. She's not wise in the ways of men. I've made sure she didn't have the chance to meet many."

"I think a lot of Doris. I'm a senior, third in my class and I'm going places. When Doris graduates in four years, I'm going to marry her," Dwayne spoke up.

"Well, I think of Victoria Principal a lot, but I doubt we're getting married," Daddy joked.

"Oh, we'll get married. I knew it the first time I saw her. I'll marry her or I'll never marry anyone," Dwayne said boldly.

Dwayne had told Tom that this statement seemed to warm the big man. He had slowly looked at his friends, and to Dwayne's mind, they almost nodded approval. Dwayne had told Tom, that he often wondered if a certain situation was luck or fate. Dwayne told Tom that this was one of those moments.

Just two days before this meeting with Big Daddy, the Judge's Will had been read. Most of the assets had gone to Timmy, but Dwayne was still shocked when he learned that he was to receive one hundred thousand dollars, ten acres of good pasture, and a large horse barn in fine shape, which was not more than six years old, on the property. He also received the Judge's grandmother's engagement and wedding rings. Now this was not just any engagement ring. It was one hundred fifty years old. Bought with slave money, no doubt. It was huge and beautiful; twenty-two carat gold, the stones were twelve diamonds and each could have been the lone stone for a ring to be proud of at today's prices. These twelve stones surrounded a stone as large as a robin's egg. A huge flawless emerald.

"Look son," Big Daddy continued, "you seem to mean well, but you're too young to talk of marriage."

"No offense sir, but I'm a young man that knows what he's doing. I've got many good opportunities opening to me. I'll make the most of them. She'll be happy, loved, and probably very spoiled."

Dwayne told Tom that he must have said something right, because now the big man was smiling and his entourage was nodding knowingly at each other, trying to stifle smiles.

Dwayne continued talking to Daddy. "I'll not interfere with her schooling. She'll graduate and then she'll come to me. She will wear white at her wedding, and for all the right reasons. We're deeply in love. I know it seems sudden and probably shocking, but it's true."

"What church do you use?" Daddy asked.

"Baptist, Sir."

"First Baptist or Southern Baptist?"

"Southern Baptist, Sir."

"Are you involved or do you just visit on Sunday?"

"I was in the choir for five years, folks said we were the best in the state," Dwayne replied.

"Well, that's something. But I want my girl to have the best."

"I am the best."

"How's that?" Daddy asked.

"It's embarrassing to explain yourself in front of strangers," Dwayne said.

"Hell boy, these ain't strangers. These men have known Doris since she was born. Each one of them loves her like they love their own children. They are family and if you ever hurt that child, you'd be seeing all of us, real quick. I'm not trying to scare you off. This is just the fact of the matter. So you don't be embarrassed. You just explain why you think you are the best."

"Well, sir, I'm smart, third in my class, a 3.9 average over four years. I volunteer at the hospital in town one night a week. I help some players on the team with their studies, tutor, you know. I'm still embarrassed to say this but I will. When I get married, I won't have known any other woman, in the biblical sense."

"Is that so?"

"Yes, Sir."

"Sounds too good to be true," said Big Daddy. "Do you think you can wait four years for a wife, that's a long time for a young man."

"I could wait forty for Doris, if I had to."

Dwayne said that the old Rams defensive line was definitely warming up. The father was glowing after this statement. Dwayne told Tom that it had to be fate and at this moment, he withdrew the package from his pocket.

"Sir, with your permission, I'm going to ask your daughter to accept this engagement ring."

"Good Lord, son, is that thing real? Thomas, look at that ring. Thomas is a jeweler. That ring real Thomas?"

Thomas looked at the ring, producing an eyeglass, magically. He was a man of few words. He said, "The ring is old, very well made. The diamonds are first quality, the emerald is flawless, I've never seen a ring this nice, outside of a museum."

The big man smiled. "Did you go into hock for that?"

"No, Sir, I've got money and ten acres of pasture in the best county in Mississippi. I've had a large windfall, enough for a good start for us."

"Well, Doris has told me she loves you, and I would never stand in her way. If she says yes, I say yes. I'll be disappointed if she marries before she's finished school."

"Well, let's call Doris out here and see what she says," Dwayne said.

Doris had been called out, and Dwayne had fallen to a knee in front of the big men and asked the question. She had looked at Daddy, and got a smile and a nod. Then, she accepted the ring. They had waited for Doris to graduate, and she had worn white at the wedding, for all the right reasons.

Dwayne and Doris had come close to making love a few times, but Dwayne had meant what he had told her father. Of course, remembering the men in that kitchen had been a great help.

Tom wondered why he had never married. When was it going to happen for him?

Chapter Eleven

"Can you think of anyone she had an argument with, lately?" Tom asked.

"No, I can't imagine anyone. She was a happy girl. Last year we talked almost every day. We were closer than we'd been for a long time. She would have told me." The mother sobbed.

"I think that's all the questions I have ma'am. We're going to find out what happened to your daughter," Tom said.

"I hope so, she was just getting her life in shape."

"Just one more question, please."

"Yes?"

"Why were you so close this year? I get the impression there was a separation of some sort?"

"Jane had a drinking problem. She took after her father, there. God bless him. Oh, No! I'll have to remember to say God bless them, now, won't I?

"Yes, ma'am," Tom said. "She'd stopped drinking?"

"Oh, yes. I didn't say, did I? She had gone to detox, and this time, she followed the doctor's orders. She joined AA. She went to a meeting every day. She really loved being sober and she was meeting so many nice people at the meetings."

"Thank you, Mrs. Comfort, Officer Clark will drive you home. We will call you with any developments. Feel free to call me anytime. My home number is on this card."

"Goodbye, Lieutenant."

Tom reached into his jacket for a cigarette. He disliked, no, not disliked, dreaded talking to a victim's family. Some cases were different. The families were the suspects. A case like this though, no way was a family member the killer. Tom thought to himself, if it were a family member it would be extremely unusual.

He had stopped at the station hoping that maybe Dan had identified the woman. He had let it be known that he thought a call would be coming about a missing woman, about 36 years old. Sure enough, the call came in and found its way to him.

The victim had definitely had a life. She was very well kept. He knew she'd be missed. Sadly, this wasn't always true. Now, he had a name to go with the body, Jane Comfort.

The name itself seemed to mock him. Jane Comfort. He felt bad. She hadn't died in comfort. The scene of the crime evoked many words, but comfort wasn't one of them.

He hadn't slept last night and fatigue was catching him. Three hours sleep would do the trick. He had an idea, but he doubted he could find his man at home before six o'clock. Sleep now; that was the ticket.

Chapter Twelve

J im was on the roof now, just capping it off. He was always happy when he was capping. That was the last part of shingling a roof. Payday, he thought. Maybe I'll try the roulette at the Sands tonight. He'd really clobbered them last week. Maybe his luck had held. Yeah, he felt lucky. Tonight . . . the Sands.

He decided to go home and sleep until about ten o'clock. Then he would head down to Atlantic City. It didn't pay to go when the casino was crowded. You couldn't follow the board; you'd miss numbers. Late night roulette was his game. Maybe Patty would go with him. Patty was a natural born loser, at the tables. Jim liked to take her along. Numbers she bet on, he stayed away from. It worked fairly well; he laughed as he remembered her 'I just lost it all' look. He never met anyone who was so dedicated to the wheel with such bad luck.

Jim had met Patty at A. A. when they both used to go. They didn't go to meetings anymore. He didn't drink anymore, but he was sure he would if he'd gone to many more meetings.

People had joked at meetings. If you were a thief before you came to AA, now you'd be a better thief. If you were an accountant, now you'd be a better accountant. If you were a hooker, now you'd be a better hooker. People laughed when they heard this theory exposed. He didn't. He'd gone to meetings a long time. He saw that it was true.

Anyhow, the meetings used to be for drunks like him. Anymore, you had heroin addicts at the meetings; acidheads, who never really drank at all; crack heads, who never recovered, except a few, very few. Lately, the AA rooms were being used as baby-sitting services for halfway houses. A van would pull up to a meeting, loaded with residents of these houses. Alcohol wasn't their problem, he thought, they shouldn't be there. They would mumble to themselves during the entire meeting. They would interrupt anyone for a cigarette, a soda, a cookie, a doughnut. Hell, they thought meetings were picnics.

He'd had his fill of it. Just don't drink. Two years this had worked for him. He didn't think about drinking anymore. When he was attending the meetings that was all he thought about. Looking at the van people, drugged up to the max, so they would be easier to handle, and the low junkies, sober but still junkies, he had decided that he'd had his last meeting. He was certain of that.

Patty drank now, but not too bad. Tonight he'd play roulette. He was happy. No more roofing this week. No more meetings, ever. He couldn't be certain he would win at the tables, but he would have bet the three grand he just slipped into his pocket that he wouldn't be at a meeting tonight. He would have lost that bet.

Chapter Thirteen

J im woke up slowly. Hard work did this to him, lately. Twenty years ago, he had roofed houses, drunk all night, had a cup of coffee, then put on another roof. No more, he was pushing fifty and the work told on him. Sleep was important now, but Lex, his Rottweiler, had put an end to his rest. Lex was raising hell down at the door. He knew he had to go downstairs, before the dog chewed the knob off the door.

His first thought was "cops". Couldn't be, he realized, as he put his feet on the floor. He hadn't been arrested since he quit drinking. Booze and jail went together for him. He was a good guy when he was sober. He was entirely someone else when he was drunk. More than once, the cops had awakened him. Usually, there had been a brawl, someone was really hurt, and he was it. Jim remembered how frustrating it was trying to defend himself, when he couldn't even remember the last three bars he was in. Blackouts had made him get sober. He had awakened too many times with bruises on his face and blood on his shirt, and no idea what had happened.

"I must be psychic," Jim said.

"Jimbo, can I come in?" Tom asked.

"Yeah, come on in. Lex, shut up, go lay down."

"Where did you get that monster?"

"He's no monster, he's my baby. Come on Lex, give me kisses."

The dog wagged his stub of a tail and soaked Jim's face. Jim told him to go lay down and he did.

"Jim, I need your help," Tom said.

"Hey! That's a switch, what's up?" said Jim.

"I've got a victim, a murdered girl. I spoke to her mother, who told me that they didn't have much contact with each other until last year. She can't imagine who would have wanted to kill her daughter. I'm hoping you can fill me in on her history," said Tom.

"Jesus, Tom, Did I know her?"

"I don't know, Jim."

"You must think that I might have known her. Why me?"

"I thought you could have known her, she was an AA member."

"Tom, it's been two years since I've been to a meeting; unless she's an old timer, I wouldn't know her. How long had she been sober?" Jim asked.

"Just a year, according to her mother."

"Hell, I don't think I would have known her. What's her name?" asked Jim.

"Her name was Jane Comfort," said Tom.

"Jesus, Sweet Jane."

"Then you did know her?" Tom asked excitedly.

"Yeah, I went to meetings with her years ago. But she went back out drinking. I haven't seen her in four years. Hell, I never thought she'd get sober."

"Well, she did."

Jim looked at Tom suspiciously. "Don't ask me what I think you're going to ask me."

"Look, you know those people. Just sniff around for a while, maybe you'll kick something up."

"You mean tonight, don't you?" said Jim.

"Gotta strike while the iron's hot," said Tom.

"Shit, Tom. I was going to the casino tonight," Jim lamented.

"What's more important?"

"Ah, shit."

"I knew you'd do it for me, you never forget a favor," Tom said.

"All right, already. I owe ya. I'll do it, give me a smoke and let me make coffee. I'll tell you what I know about Jane. Jesus, Jane, she was really a nice lady."

Tom glanced around the living room. "Jim, this place is a wreck."

"I like it like that, clear a seat, it's messy, but it's clean. The dog tears up everyday and I haven't cleaned up since yesterday. It's my fault, though. He needs a woman, 'Don't you Lexy'. His hormones are driving him crazy. I'm going to the kennels to get him a wife. Then I'll be selling little Lexes, won't I boy?"

"Do you think two dogs will be less mess?" Tom asked.

"Oh, I know it. He'll walk around all day with his nose up her ass. She'll walk the floors trying to get a minutes rest. Believe me, as far as housekeeping is concerned, two are less trouble than one."

"And the puppies?"

Jim laughed, "Now that's a really shitty story, but I'll spare you the details."

Jim poured coffee for both of them. He liked Tom. He had gotten Jim out of an assault charge, bar fight. The only condition of his probation was AA meetings for a year. He'd gotten his life together at AA. But he had outgrown the meetings after a few years. Too many weirdoes were in the rooms now. Definitely, no one he'd seen in the bars, either, and he'd hit all the bars in the area at one time or another.

"Tom, I guess it was ninety-three when I first saw Jane. She came strolling into the meeting; man she was one hot looking woman. I tried to tell her to stay out of any kind of relationship for the first year, but she hooked up with some scum bag right out of the gate."

Jim continued. "We talked a lot. Hell, I think I was in love with her. She was more than beautiful; she was really alive. She got well way too fast. Heck, after she attended meetings for about six months, she thought she knew it all. She got pregnant, but she never had the baby. She just stopped showing up, which usually means, back to the bottle."

"She earned a living as a dancer, not at the shitty clubs on the Boulevard, but the high class clubs. You know, four dollars a beer, all suits. I never went to those clubs. The way I drank, if a beer was more than a buck, I was gone," Jim laughed.

"Anyway, last I heard, the scumbag left her after maxing out her credit cards. Maybe she moved in with another dancer. Anyway, that was the impression that I was left with."

"This 'scumbag'," Tom asked, "was he the father of the baby?"

"Yeah, that was it. She was upset about having an abortion; she didn't want to do it. But the scumbag didn't want to lose her income, which he considered to be his income, while she took time to have a baby. He talked her into it. She was smart, but not street smart, if you know what I mean."

"Do you remember his name, the scumbag?" Tom asked.

"Oh, yeah. His name was Lenny A."

Tom looked incredulous, "Lenny A.? That's all you've got for me?"

"It's supposed to be an "anonymous" program, Tom. If I ever did know his last name, I've forgotten it," said Jim.

"You out of coffee?" Tom said, looking toward the kitchen.

"You want a cup, just say so."

"I want a cup."

"So, okay then."

Jim poured more coffee. He tried to remember the punk's last name, but no joy.

"Aren't there membership lists that people sign when they join?" Tom asked.

"No way man. You're a member if you say you're a member. Lot's of drunks drive to a meeting, far, far away from their homes. People don't want to give their name. You can understand that."

"Well, that makes sense, I guess. Maybe you can see if the scumbag has resurfaced," Tom suggested.

"You think he's good for it, don't you?" Jim asked.

"It might fit."

"Let me dust off my leathers and get the Harley out. If I get any information, I'll call you."

"That's what I was counting on. I think if I tried to sneak into a meeting and ask questions, everyone would clam up," said Tom.

"They'd know you were a cop in three seconds."

"Yeah, they would, I know. But your biker look, that helps people open up, doesn't it?"

"People trust bikers. They figure you're such a fuck up they can tell you anything, it never fails," said Jim.

"Good luck tonight, Jim. Call me as soon as you get home. I want to know whatever you hear, even if it doesn't sound like it fits. Anything strange. We're going after "strange" here. Whoever did this is not close to normal. Weird, think weird.

Jim chuckled, "That's the only way I think."

"I know, that's why I'm here."

Tom drove away thinking it was a long shot, but a shot's a shot. The real work would begin tomorrow.

Jim watched Tom leave. He had Tom to thank for everything he had. He'd find out for Tom and for Jane, if there were indeed, anything to find out.

Chapter Fourteen

J im waited until seven-thirty, then he climbed on the Harley and headed toward a church, where he thought there might be a meeting tonight. He still had the itch to gamble, and he wasn't in a good mood. He blasted his way through the streets. He hadn't been on the bike in quite a while; it was still a kick in the ass. He was feeling better. He'd try to be in a better mood.

There were cars at the church. The bumper stickers would tell if it was an AA bunch. He pulled into the lot. Oh, hell, yeah. The stickers on the bumpers were there. An old Cadillac's sticker declared that it was a "Friend of Bill W". Another on a new Bronco recommended, "Easy Does It". They were here, the Early Birds, making coffee and setting up chairs. He knew ninety percent of the people at the meetings were dedicated, good people. He couldn't accept the ten-percent crazies and schemers.

He parked and walked into the church. He got coffee and had a seat in the back. Man, this was going to be a long hour and a half.

"Hey, Jim, welcome back!"

"Mike, how you doing?" Jim responded.

"Still making meetings."

"That's good, Mike."

"Look, Jim, I've got to talk to Tony, he's struggling," Mike said apologetically.

"So go! Who's stopping ya?"

Jim had liked Mike at one time, but he had gotten to know him too well. That's why he stopped going to meetings. He knew these people, too well. He'd been drunk the better part of twenty years, but he had a lot of nevers. He'd never robbed his friends. He'd never slept with his brother's wife. He'd never beat a baby up in a drunken rage. But he knew these people, and some of them had done these things. They were accepted here and the things they had done were understood and forgiven by the mainstream people at the meetings. Not by Jim, though. He thought that if you beat a baby, it didn't have anything to do with being drunk. He thought that person was just a low-down, good-for-nothing, rat.

"Yo! Margie," Jim called.

"Oh, my God."

"How are you, girl?" Jim asked.

"I'm great. Where have you been? We all heard you're drinking again, but I'm glad to see you. One day at a time."

"Margie, I'm not drinking, who told you that bullshit? Never mind. It doesn't matter. Listen, step outside with me. I need to ask you something."

"I'll go outside with you Jim, but remember, the only shame is to stop trying."

Jim got up to walk outside with Margie. She was a dedicated AA nut. He knew that he could tell her a hundred times that he hadn't been drinking, but she wouldn't believe it. She was sure that everyone who stopped attending meetings, immediately fell back to the bottle. Jim thought that he'd leave her with her illusions. She had been a hopeless drunk and maybe she would fall back into the bottle, if she stopped making meetings. Jim was sure she would. AA was her whole life.

"Margie, when was the last time you saw Sweet Jane?" he asked.

"Jane C?" Margie asked.

"Yeah, Jane C."

"She's supposed to meet me here tonight."

Stupid bitch, Jim thought. He remembered now, how hard it was to talk to Margie. She never answered a question. She'd always try to figure out why you asked the question and answer the "why". She hadn't had a drink in twenty years, but he was still talking to someone who was wet. That is, someone who drank so much, they would never think straight.

"Margie, when was the last time you saw Sweet Jane?" he tried again.

"She should be here any minute, she'll be glad to see you."

"Thanks, Margie. I guess I'll just wait here to say hello to Jane. Hey, I think they're calling the meeting to order."

"Yes, they are. Jim, aren't you coming in?"

"No, Margie. I'm not ready yet. You better go, though. Don't want to be late."

"That's right Jim, somebody might say something that will help me get another day sober. Meeting makers make it, Jim. I expect to see you inside. Bye bye."

Jim watched Margie rush into the church for the meeting. God bless that burned out nut. Well, she didn't know about Jane, that's for sure. He knew she was one of the main stems of the AA grapevine. Maybe nobody knew.

He watched a cab pull into the lot.

"Hi, Jim, welcome back."

"Hi, Ron," Jim said flatly.

"So what have you been doing?" Ron asked.

"Ron, fuck off. You're a creep and I never liked ya," Jim said.

"He stays sober though, doesn't He?" the cabby said.

"Start walking asshole or I'll drop ya right here," said Jim.

"Temper, temper! Got a little hangover there?" Ron smiled.

Jim jumped off the bike and headed for Ron.

"Alright, He's going in. You need help," said the cabby.

Now he remembered why he didn't make meetings. He did have a short temper, and more than once he'd wanted to punch one of these idiots.

Margie can't answer a question. Ron was happy at the meetings. Why people liked someone who referred to himself as "He", he couldn't begin to guess. The guy made his skin crawl. The prevailing feeling at the meeting was that if you stay sober, everything else is unimportant. Jim couldn't accept that.

Damn it, I'm not going to learn anything here. Jim thought he'd take a ride for about an hour. The diner at the circle would be his next stop, after the meeting. Lots of the folks in the meetings went there for coffee and bullshit after the meetings. He'd learn more there in half an hour, than he'd get in an hour and a half in the church. He climbed on the bike.

He was grateful to be sober, more grateful that he could do it without these nuts. He kicked the bike to life and rolled out of the lot.

Jim thought of the creep. Why didn't he ever say "I"? "He" stays sober, doesn't "He"? Who talks like that? What an asshole! Jim thought he should give Ron's name to Tom. Not because he thought he did anything, but because he really disliked the weirdo. But, Tom didn't want a room full of suspects just because Jim didn't like them. Still, it was tempting. Ron was a creep. Jim knew that the list of people he didn't like was long. Jim didn't like many people, and most people didn't like Jim.

He'd ride over to Philly and kill the hour. Anyway, the freaks on South Street were always amusing.

Chapter Fifteen

Yesterday had been a good day for Dwayne and his family. Doris and Daddy were his whole family. He caught them before they left the condo. Doris wasn't steering Daddy toward the mall. It was to be the outlets up in Reading. Dwayne wasn't crazy about shopping, but he enjoyed watching these two. They both liked it, and they were funny to watch. The drive out through Pennsylvania was beautiful and they laughed a lot on the trip to and from the outlets.

It was Tuesday morning. Dwayne's thoughts turned to the murder case. He'd jog around the river, shower and head up to the Lantern. He hoped someone had come up with something. He couldn't think of any angle that made sense, aside from the aborted child, angry over theory. That had to be it. We had to find out who the father was. It was probably that simple.

Alice was starting her shift at the Lantern. It was early, but the place was about half full. It only had ten seats and they stayed full almost all day. She was feeding Sammy, the guy that collected beer and soda cans. She liked him, and he liked her. Sammy was short, usually dirty, but always in a good mood. The cops chipped in once a month to get Sammy a room for a week, so he could rest safely and clean up. Alice knew Sammy did okay in the summer, but she worried about him in the winter. Sammy slept rough most of the time.

"Well," Alice thought, "He'll get a good breakfast as long as I'm working here." She always fed Sammy early, then pushed him toward his bike. She made sure he'd eaten plenty and usually gave him a fried egg sandwich for later. She often wondered how old he was, but it was impossible to tell. He was old, just old. He never spoke a word. Alice wondered if he ever could.

Poor little bastard, she thought. She was playing with the idea of taking him home to live with her, but she knew it was crazy.

"You still feeding that bum?"

"Good morning to you too, Ready," she said.

"What's good about it?"

"Well, the sun is shining and the air is fresh."

"And you're smiling like you're responsible for it."

"Ready, I like you and I'm in a good mood, but I'd really like you to do me a favor today."

"What's that, Alice? I probably won't do it, but what is it?"

"Shut up!"

"I told you I wouldn't do it," Ready laughed.

"I knew it was too much to ask, where's the uniform and the dog? You on vacation?" Alice asked.

"Feels like it, but no. The Lieutenant wanted me for a special assignment. The brass know a tough case calls for the best."

"And that's you?"

"Who else, Honey?"

"Me!" Willis answered.

"You! Tom asked you to go plainclothes, too?" Ready questioned.

"Well, Ready, you did say he asked for the best," Alice laughed.

Willis walked in and sat down next to Ready, they clammed up. Alice knew the small talk would be scarce. These two really didn't like each other.

"Ready, the regular," Alice said, as she laid down one scrambled egg and ham.

"You on a diet, Ready?" Willis asked.

"No, but you might want to think about it."

"I've been on one for six months, I'm down to 410. I feel strong."

"That's great, we need any heavy lifting done today, be sure to point that out," quipped Ready.

"What kind of a remark is that, Ready? I guess you think a black man is only good for heavy lifting."

"I wondered how long it would take you," said Ready.

"What do you mean?" Willis asked.

"Not this shit again!" Alice shouted. "Not this morning and not in here. Damn it, I'll have you both out sitting on the curb."

"Wait a minute, Alice. You're forgetting about the First Amendment," Willis reminded her.

"That's right, Alice. 'We, the people,'" Ready added.

"You two! Two peas in a pod," Alice stated.

"I ain't no pea in his damn pod," Willis corrected.

"Nor I in his," Ready mocked.

"Nor I in his," Willis said. "You think that fancy talk impresses me. I'll debate your dumb ass anytime."

"Two peas in a pod," Alice said. "Willis, what are you having? Ready, no cracks."

"Eggs, pancakes and O.J." Willis said.

"Yeah, Alice, I haven't had any O.J. since the trial. I just can't swallow it," Ready said.

"Oh, I guess that's a come back," Willis said.

"The jury found the man 'not guilty', but I guess that isn't good enough for you," Willis said.

"Why'd they find him 'not guilty'?" Ready asked.

"For a lot of reasons, called evidence."

"No, seriously, Willis?"

"I am serious. For one thing, the gloves. "If they don't fit you must acquit." Case closed. Not guilty!

"Hey, Alice, you ever throw a pair of wet gloves down?"

"Sure, so?"

"What happened when you tried to put them on six months later?" Ready asked.

"Usually they didn't fit. If they had any leather on them, they shrunk."

"They were smaller, of course. But people in Los Angeles don't wear gloves as a habit. Maybe they didn't know this," said Ready.

"The jury found him 'not guilty'. You can talk until you retire, but that's what's up your nose. I'm eating."

"You two should be a lot of fun to work with. I'm so happy for Tom," Alice said.

Just then, Dwayne stepped into the Lantern. "Hi, Alice. Morning, guys," he said.

"Hey, Dwayne. What's it going to be?" said Alice.

"Just oatmeal and toast, no coffee, O.J., please."

Alice quickly glanced and Ready and Willis. "You two don't get started again."

Tom had followed closely behind Dwayne. He waited for his coffee. He didn't feel like talking yet. He lit a cigarette.

"Tom, since when?" Alice asked, looking at his cigarette.

"A day or two," Tom said.

"It's tough," Alice said as she took a drag of her Newport.

The coffee was strong and Tom began to wake up. He wondered what Willis and Ready were talking about when he came in.

"So what's everyone talking about, Alice?" Tom asked.

"A lot of nothing, these two. You're going to work with both of them all day?"

"For a month, maybe," Tom said.

"I'll go to church and light a candle."

"Thanks Alice, you think I'll need it?" Tom asked.

"Will you need it? We've already had the trial of O.J. in here, and there's a whole day ahead."

"Not guilty! That's right." Willis said.

"I've got a different case on my mind today men, but we can all relax and enjoy our breakfasts."

"Tom, O.J.! Guilty or not guilty?" Ready shouted down the counter.

"Jury said, 'not guilty' that's good enough for me," Tom said. It was not what he believed, but he wanted to burn Ready's ass.

Willis laughed, "Oh, you don't look too happy, Ready."

Ready kept his nose in the cup, drinking his coffee, but you could see that he was steamed.

Tom was trying to keep a straight face and it wasn't too tough this early. He had taken Willis's side and Ready was sulking like a big baby. He knew how to cheer him up, though. Dwayne hadn't heard the *Martin Luther King Day bet*. Tom thought back to the time when this bet originated, seventy or seventy-one? A long time ago.

"Dwayne," Tom said, "The whole thing between these guys started twenty-seven years ago, when they were rookies. There was some bet that they made. Hey, guys, who won that bet?"

"I won that bet. Easy money, common sense," Ready bragged.

"Common sense? Where's the common sense?" Willis asked.

"Wait a minute guys, if you're going to discuss this I really feel you should consider Dwayne, and start from the beginning," Tom urged.

"Suits me," Willis said.

"You never paid up," Ready said.

"I paid up. I left it in your locker."

"I never got it," Ready said.

Willis's face reddened. "I watched you walk to your locker. One minute later, you got it."

"I would remember that," Ready said.

"We are getting old, I guess you could be senile."

Dwayne's curiosity was aroused now. "What was the bet?" he asked.

"I'll tell it," Ready said.

"Tell it right," Willis warned.

"What else! Here goes. Me and Willis there are watching the news during a break in training at the station. John Facenda comes on the set. He says, "They're going to announce which day of the year will be dedicated as *Martin Luther King Day*. So I say to Willis, "That's easy to pick."

Willis says to me, "How's that?"

"Well, I say, the Federal guys down in Washington will just pick the coldest day of the year."

Willis chimes in, "And I said, 'they wouldn't do something mean like that.'"

"And then I said, 'Down there in Washington, them good old boys on the Hill ain't gonna risk a summer barbecue turning into a riot."

"And I said to Ready, 'Oh, a white barbecue never turned into a riot?'"

"Then I said, 'Willis, they just don't want to risk a nationwide barbecue breaking into a riot. I know how them old boys think. It will be one of the coldest days of the year. I'll bet you one hundred dollars.'"

"And I said, 'The money is covered.'"

Dwayne frowned, "That was the bet?"

"That was it," Willis said glumly.

"*Martin Luther King Day* is January 17 or 18, isn't it? Ready won the bet. There couldn't be a much colder date," Dwayne said.

"Yeah, I think that date was selected for just the reasons Ready gave," Willis said.

"Yup, yup, back in the old days, you could trust our boys in Washington," Ready smiled.

"*You* could," Willis said.

"Come on guys, Willis and Ready same car. Meet us at the park by the boats, we'll talk," Tom said.

Breakfast was officially over. Ready wasn't sulking.

Chapter Sixteen

Tuesday Afternoon.

It was Tuesday afternoon and Tom and Dwayne had been talking over the case. It was a good first day and they were tired. The footwork was going well, but no suspect yet. Dwayne had talked to friends of the victim. Officer Clark had a list that was offered by Mrs. Comfort. That list had produced another list. The second list was covered pretty well.

"Ready and Willis should be here any minute," Tom said.

"More of the same probably, no one has any idea who would do something like this."

"Considering this lady was a dancer, she led a surprisingly boring life." Tom was surprised, too. She'd dance by day and got drunk at night and she drank at home and alone. She drank a lot. Until a year ago, then she got sober again.

The records of the abortion had been studied. The name of the father found, Lenny Allison. But that became a dead end when a computer check found that he had been dead since New Years Eve. He had fallen asleep, drunk, in a friend's driveway. He had frozen to death. The main suspect was certainly eliminated.

"If we can't turn up a weird one who was close to her, personally involved with the victim, we have to start thinking random killer, don't we?" Dwayne asked.

Tom looked at Dwayne while he spoke, but just dropped his head back toward the papers on his lap. Tom just realized something. Something Jim had said. He'd said, "I was in love with her." Or, something close. Tom couldn't discount anyone. It did fit. He wondered if Jim had ever gone out with her and he wondered where Jim was on Saturday night. Jim wasn't the type. It couldn't be, but Tom was a cop. He had to check it out. Tom thought what a crummy friend a cop could be.

"I don't buy random," Tom said.

"It's possible, isn't it?" Dwayne asked.

"Anything's possible, but this guy was there with flowers. The flowers and the mutilation say this was about abortion. I'm thinking, maybe a friend whose girl had an abortion. He can't get at her. He finds out Jane had an abortion and he lets her sit in for his girl."

"Could be, looks better now that we know the father is dead," Dwayne said.

"But who? We are back to 'who'!" Tom said.

"Maybe someone who watched her dance."

"Maybe Willis will know. He's probably covered every club she worked at," said Tom.

"Tom, do you think those two really hate each other?" Dwayne asked.

"No, I don't think so. Their heads are just stuck in the sixties. I think they just like to argue."

"It's a good act, they could take it on stage," Dwayne laughed.

"Yeah, they could, couldn't they," Tom agreed.

"You know, we've got to remember that we are looking for someone who spent about four hundred dollars on props," Dwayne said.

"A bike, satin sheets and flowers," Tom mused. "A customer at an expensive dance club would have that kind of money to throw away."

"That's right," Dwayne said. "Beer is five bucks a bottle."

"I heard four from Jim, but he hasn't been drinking for a while."

"What about your roofer pal, think he'll come up with anything?"

"I'm worried he might be a suspect," Tom said.

"What? And you sent him out looking around?" Dwayne asked.

"It just hit me a minute ago. When I was at his house, he said something like *he was in love with her once*. But I didn't get the impression he meant a relationship, more of a crush. I wish I could remember exactly how he put it."

"How well do you know him?"

"How well do you know anybody, friend or not, until I know where he was Saturday night . . . oh, well," Tom shook his head.

"Does he have money to burn?" Dwayne asked.

"Jim's a crude guy. He's got an old saying. 'He works like a dog to live like a pig.'"

"What's that mean?" Dwayne asked.

"He breaks his ass, making good money roofing, but throws a lot of it away at the tables."

"Gambling can cause a lot of problems for people, Tom."

"Yeah, I'll check on his alibi, but he's not the type."

"What type is he?" asked Dwayne.

"That's a tough question. He's rough, short tempered, intelligent, but he tries hard to hide it. Loves animals, not crazy about too many people. But he's a good friend if you're in a jam. If he were angry, he'd just go off at somebody. No way is it him. The guy that did this is a sneak and a coward. Someone who holds in his anger. Probably a trouble maker who always stays out of the trouble."

"Well that narrows the suspects. Looking for one trouble maker with money," Dwayne said.

"Dwayne, I know you're joking, but let's think about what you just said," said Tom.

"Okay, a trouble maker with some money. I'll remember it, but we need a place to hang it," said Dwayne.

"That will come. Let's just try and remember it. This case is going to be patched together. We're going to need every piece," said Tom.

"It's in the mental file," Dwayne said. "But the roofer doesn't look good?"

"No way, but I'll check."

"How close are you two, Tom?"

"Not that close."

"Here's Willis and Ready," Dwayne said.

Willis and Ready drove into the park and pulled up next to Tom and Dwayne. Tom had to smile. They were still arguing.

"Let me out of this stinking car!" Ready said, as he jumped out.

Willis shut the motor off and was laughing with his head on the wheel.

"What's his problem, Willis?" Tom asked.

"He's white," Willis said and broke up laughing.

"That's no problem, that's a blessing. I'll tell you my problem Lieutenant. Garbage Gut ate six bean burritos for lunch, and he's been sharing them with me ever since," Ready said.

"Gas, Tom. I can't help it," Willis laughed.

"He ate 'em on purpose," Ready yelled.

"If I didn't know better, I'd think I was listening to a couple of rookies," Tom laughed.

"You weren't in the car; he's disgusting."

Willis was having a good time. The angrier Ready got, the harder Willis laughed.

"Let's walk gentlemen, we can talk things over. Willis stay down wind, okay?" Tom said.

"So what have you two got beside gas?" Dwayne asked.

"I don't have gas," Ready said.

"Knock it off. So what's up? Anything?"

"Well," Willis said, "she seems like a loner. The bartenders said pretty much the same thing. She stayed to herself, except for one period while she was with a guy named Lenny. No trouble, no drugs, but they all had the impression she drank. Never while she was working, but a bartender can tell when he's talking to someone who drinks. They were pretty sure she did."

"A couple of guys were nuts for her at the clubs. But the same guys went nuts for whoever was dancing the next day." No groupies," Ready said.

"That's right, Boss, she was all work at the clubs, no play. She always got an escort to her car, someone who worked at the club, she left alone."

"Did they say she ever seemed scared?" Tom asked.

"Nothing like that," Willis said.

"So more nothing," Tom said.

"I guess so, Tom," Willis said.

"Look! It's as plain as the nose on your face, the boy friend," Ready said.

"He's been dead six months," Dwayne said.

"Ready wouldn't let him off the hook for that," Willis needled.

"I've got to believe that somebody has some idea who did this," Tom said. "We're just not looking in the right places."

"Tomorrow at the Lantern, at 7 a.m. Take off guys; we'll see you then. I've got something to check out," Tom said.

"Ready, you getting in?" Willis asked.

"I live three blocks away. I can walk."

"If that's how you want it," Willis drove off laughing.

"Tom, maybe if Willis and I split up we can cover more ground," Ready said.

"I'll think about it Ready, it might be a good idea."

"See you tomorrow, men," Ready said as he headed up a hill toward his home.

"You going to split them up?" Dwayne asked.

"No."

"I didn't think so."

Chapter Seventeen

Tom got Jim's number out of the classified section of the paper. 'Roofing and Siding call Jim.' He dialed the number.

"Hello," Jim answered.

"Hey Jim, it's Tom, you gonna be there a while?"

"I'll be here, come on over."

Tom didn't feel good about what he had to ask Jim. But he didn't have a sterling record and you never excluded anyone for personal reasons.

Tom had one more call to make. This one was to Shelly, and he felt uncomfortable about what he was going to ask her to do. All she can say is "no".

"Hello."

"Hello Shelly, it's Tom."

"I know your voice, Tom."

"Oh, yeah, of course you do, anyway, the reason I called is that we're having trouble getting the history, anything really personal, about the victim. I still only have a vague idea who she was. Now, don't be afraid to say no, this might be a stupid idea if I thought more about it."

"Let's hear it Tom. I'm intrigued."

"Well Shelly, if a girl went to the clubs and got close to the other dancers, maybe they would know something we don't know about Jane Comfort."

"Tom, are you suggesting I dance in a strip club?" asked Shelly.

"Hell no, Shelly. No! No! Just act like you're considering it, maybe. You could tell a dancer Jane was a friend of yours and maybe you'd learn something."

"It might be interesting," Shelly said.

"You'll do it?" Tom asked.

"Why not? But I'll come up with my own methods."

"What's wrong with the potential dancer line?"

"Sounds like a girl in trouble."

"So what; not a lot of happy girls take those jobs," Tom said.

"I'd rather talk from a position of strength."

"Such as?"

"That will be a secret. Figure it out."

"Can you meet me at the park around noon? The clubs should just be opening. You could catch the dancers before they started their sets," Tom said.

"You know about the sets, Tom?"

"Only on a professional level."

"I'll see you at noon," Shelly said.

"Goodbye, Shelly."

He knew she'd do it. Shelly had to be bored. Dan had everything wrapped up and he was turning his files over to the new man. Right about now, this was medicine for her. Tom didn't doubt she'd probably be the one to get something first. A position of strength . . . Tom thought about that as he grabbed his keys to the Jeep.

Shelly grabbed her keys on her way to the printers, a position of strength. Shelly would need a fast order and she knew just the printer. He was a homely kid, nineteen years old, a good printer and nuts about Shelly. She laughed thinking of him. He was sad, such a crush. He'd knock out her order in two hours.

She thought how perfectly Angel's Prowler would fit her plans. She'd look the part.

Tom drove to Jim's house.

"Come on in Tom, the dog's out back," Jim yelled at the front door.

"So tell me something good," Tom said.

"Not much to tell. She was expected to be at that meeting. I got it from a few people there."

"Nobody mentioned any trouble she might have had?"

"Nothing like that; they were sure she would be there. It's her home group."

"What's that, Jim?" Tom asked.

"That's like a group you belong to where you are responsible for having the coffee ready, keeping the place clean, like that."

"You see or hear anything or anybody strange?"

"Hell, everybody's strange. But I did hear something at the diner; it's probably nothing."

"It might be, give," said Tom.

"Well, one guy from the meeting didn't make it home from work last night. A new guy at the meeting has just been at his house one day. They just met Sunday at another meeting. He said this guy, Marco, let him stay at his house, but Marco never came home from work. Marco told him he was going to the meeting at the church by the tire center. So the kid's at the meeting, wondering if he should go back to Marco's or what.

"What do you think's up?" Tom asked.

"He probably fell off the wagon, happens all the time," Jim said.

"Keep your ears open, if this Marco doesn't pop up, let me know."

"Wait a minute Tom, this was a one time deal, right?" Jim said.

"Come on, hang around a while with these people. It won't hurt too bad."

"I don't think it will help," Jim replied.

"But we don't know, do we?"

"Jesus Tom, I'll do it but it really stinks."

"This is my night to be a stinker, I guess."

"What else do I have to do?"

"Just tell me where you were Saturday night."

"Oh, this is beautiful. Now I'm a suspect," said Jim.

"Jim, everyone who knew her is."

"I guess you're right; but if I were you I wouldn't have asked me."

"Sorry, but I've got to know," said Tom.

"I had a roof in Lewes, Delaware, a rip off. I was there Saturday and Sunday. I stayed at the Quality Inn on Route 1. Oh, they'll remember me; I snuck Lex into the room. He was barking Sunday morning. They gave me hell and I gave it back," said Jim.

"Sorry, but I had to ask."

"I'll go to a couple more meetings Tom, but that's it. I'll call you if I get anything. Right now, I'm going upstairs to smoke a joint. You can let yourself out."

"You're pissed, aren't you?" said Tom.

"Fucking A, I'll call ya. Now get out of my house."

Tom didn't feel too proud of himself walking back to the car. He knew Jim though; he'd get over it in five or six years. He didn't hold a grudge too long. Jim took it better than Tom thought he might. Tom knew it wasn't Jim, now he couldn't help but feel stupid. Tom knew he probably could have gotten this out of him another way. But Jim was so paranoid he'd probably have figured out what Tom was after. Jim would have been twice as angry if he sensed the sneak approach. Tom got in the car and looked at the house. He wondered if he'd ever have coffee with Jim and Lex again. He lit a cigarette and drove home. He doubted it.

Shit, Tom thought, there goes my new roof.

Chapter Eighteen

Tom parked his Jeep in the lot in front of Dwayne's condo. It was Wednesday morning, only six-thirty. He had a little trouble sleeping last night; was it the case or meeting Shelly today? He thought about it. It must be time to retire. It was Shelly. He was nervous, like a schoolboy. Tom lit a cigarette and drank his coffee. He thought about the two guys that worked for Jim. They would probably have a tough day. Well at least he wouldn't kick the dog, he loved that dog. Tom flipped his smoke into the drain in the lot, another nice day.

Dwayne watched Tom from his balcony. He was thinking about the case as he watched Tom lean against his car, stare at the river and smoke.

The smoke drifting away from Tom seemed symbolic of the case. It was spooky. He thought how strange it was to have a spooky thought on a sunny July morning.

Dwayne looked back down at Tom. He was walking to the door.

Tom said, "Good morning," to the doorman. The greeting was returned. He liked these condos; they were getting old but holding up well. In South Jersey, it's so flat, a view is rare; these places had a view. A condo like this in New York City, seventy-five miles up the turnpike, would cost four thousand a month. These were nine hundred. Best kept secret in South Jersey. There was a waiting list to get in. He should sell the house and move here, he thought. Tom smiled, thinking of pushing the lawnmower to the curb for the last time. The new people could worry about the roof.

Tom tapped his cigarette pack into his pocket. "No Smoking" signs on the elevator walls showed someone with a cigarette in his mouth. He was being lead away in handcuffs from the elevator.

Tom silently nodded his approval. A universal sign, he thought, handcuffs. As Tom entered the hallway, Dwayne was walking toward him.

"Saw me coming," Tom stated.

"Yes I did. Anything new?"

"Not really," Tom said as he pushed the button for the elevator."

"The roofer have anything?"

"He had an alibi. It checked out."

"You lose a friend?" Dwayne asked.

"Oh, yeah."

"It happens."

"Too often," said Tom.

They rode the elevator down in silence. Dwayne had wanted to know if Tom checked Jim out. It hadn't taken Tom a second to see where Dwayne was headed.

Well, he'd had *his* coffee, Tom thought.

Tom was thinking about the assignment for Willis and Ready. They had their work cut out for them. Tracing a young girl's bike was murder. Everyone sells bikes; hardware stores, variety stores, toy stores, drug stores, just everybody. But it was one of the only solid leads. He wondered how many of this model could have been sold in the last month.

They walked into the Lantern. Alice waved them to the last two seats. The article about the murder had hit the papers and the ghouls were all here. Alice had been right. A murder was good for business.

"Hi Tom, Dwayne, the regular for you two, I hope, I'm rushed off my feet," Alice said.

"Hi Alice," Dwayne said. "How about scrambled eggs and coffee?"

"Just coffee for me, Alice," Tom said.

Alice disappeared through the door to get an order. Poole was poking Tom in the arm.

"Hi Poole, how are ya?" Tom asked.

"The dancer, that your case?"

"No it's not my case."

"Come on Tom, you can tell me the details. I can keep a secret."

"Okay Poole, but we don't know anything yet. I'm expecting something big soon. I'll let you know when it happens."

"Thanks for nothing. I know it's your case. Some cops still trust me."

"Tom, it sounds like you lost another friend," Dwayne said, as old Poole walked away.

"You know what Dwayne?"

"What?"

"I don't care. These morbid people get under my skin. I'm not telling anyone what we're doing. If they don't like it, tough."

Tom didn't like it. Like sharks in a feeding frenzy for any bit of news or gore.

"I've got my coffee. I'll wait at the park. Bring Willis and Ready over when they're finished," Tom said.

"Okay Tom, a little tense today?"

"I think I am and this place isn't helping me. See ya soon."

Dwayne watched Tom leave. He was buttonholed outside the door; two cops from another district. Whatever they asked Tom, he didn't seem to like it. Tom walked toward his car.

"Dwayne, what's wrong with him?" Alice asked.

"I guess it's the case, we aren't making much progress."

"That's always sure to put him in a foul mood."

"Well Alice, it's a foul case."

Tom drove along the river to the parking lots where the sailboats were stored. He didn't like to be asked about a case he was working on for a lot of reasons.

First, it would be unprofessional to talk about it. Everyone who was asking the stupid questions should know that.

Second, it was always the same people. Tom felt they couldn't be happy unless someone else had suffered. Maybe it was natural curiosity, but he didn't think so. Nosy creeps that they are.

Tom watched the kids getting ready for sailing lessons. These were city kids some nice church or organization had sponsored for sailing lessons. Tom doubted if many of them had even been on a boat. They'd have fun but he doubted that they'd do much sailing. They were way too wound up. Tom thought it must be the water, and the long and wide grass-covered shoreline. Heck, for these kids, grass to play on was as rare as snow to play in, for the suburban kids. The first group of kids played on grass maybe three times a year. The suburban kids played in snow about three times a year. Watching the city kids on the grass, Tom thought the excitement level between the two activities about equal. Damn shame that, he thought.

Tom knew why he was uptight. It wasn't old time cops asking questions. Also, it wasn't the case. Shelly would be here, right here, at noon. That was the reason. He wasn't telling Dwayne that, though. He'd let him think other things had him bugged.

"Deep in thought, Tom?" Dwayne asked.

"I guess I was. Willis and Ready, here are pictures of the bike, make and model. Check everywhere within a ten-mile radius. I know it's a long shot, but it's a shot. Someone bought that bike, and someone sold it. I've got to believe that he bought it within the last two weeks. But don't rule out a month."

"Good morning to you, too," Willis said.

"Be looking for a guy that bought it alone, no wife, no kids, no one with him."

"Good morning, Tom," Ready said. "What's on my plate today?"

"You're with Willis."

"But Tom, I thought, you know."

"You two are good together. Now get going. I want a list of every single guy that bought that model bike. There can't be that many. Ask if they have video tape," Tom said.

"Come on, Willis. No Mexican today, alright?" Ready said.

"I don't care where we eat, let's go," Willis stated.

Dwayne watched the pair leave.

"Ready looked pissed."

"I never promised him anything."

"Why do you needle him, Tom?"

"Because he's got it coming."

"Dwayne, I've been avoiding the crime scene for a couple of reasons. First, I don't want to get us in the shithouse with the Feds. Second, I don't think we'll get anywhere there. But, maybe, if we put a couple men down there, Mag might start worrying about his stash. The men could ask everybody on the street a lot of questions, be seen a lot," Tom said.

"You're thinking that if Mag worries enough about his goods . . ."

"That's right. Who could find a creep faster than Mag? His life *is* creeps."

"Alright Tom, but we're walking a thin line," Dwayne said.

"But it's a line," Tom said.

"I just hope Mag doesn't run crying to the Feds."

"I don't think he will. I doubt if the Feds have told him they know where his stash is. As long as he's helping them, it wouldn't be to their advantage."

"I'll bet you're right!" Dwayne said. He was happy to hear this, he wasn't looking for trouble.

"Dwayne, I want you to check out the florist. Try the City, Lawnside, Gloucester, Westville, and Mt. Ephraim. I guess what I'm telling you is to check all local shops. They weren't cheap arrangements and the two together should be remembered, Lilies and Roses. Here are the pictures of the flowers. Good luck," Tom said.

"Maybe he bought one bunch here and the other there."

"Possible, I admit. Remember, a guy alone," Tom said.

"I'm just glad it's not the week after Valentine's Day," Dwayne said.

"Yeah, or Mother's Day," Tom laughed.

"I've got to talk to Jim again. I've got a feeling there might be something in what he said."

"Will he talk to you?" Dwayne asked.

"I can cool him down. He's got a conscience. I'll work on that."

"What's the deal?"

"He said some guy in AA is missing. Maybe this guy was feeling guilty. I've got to follow it up."

"Murderers have been known to rabbit," Dwayne said.

"You're damn right. The timing is about right. I'm on it this morning. I'll drive you to your house. Would you mind using your car?" Tom asked.

"Hell no, I never get to drive it."

Tom dropped Dwayne off at his condo. He thought he knew where Jim was working. Earlier this morning, Tom drove past one of Jim's signs at a house on Haddon Avenue; a dumpster was being dropped there. Every contractor in the city knew if he didn't fill his dumpster by the end of the day, everyone in the neighborhood would fill it for him, after dark. Jim would be there today, guaranteed. He'd fill his own dumpster. Tom drove off, looking at his watch. Shelly at noon. A little more than four hours. If he was getting this nervous over a meeting, how was he going to pull off a date?

He drove toward Haddon Avenue a little disgusted with himself. He knew nothing about women, well nothing much.

Chapter Nineteen

Wednesday Morning 10 a.m.

"Hey Jim, come on down!" Tom yelled up at the roofer.

"You know everything I know. Nobody told you guys to quit working," Jim said to Tom, and then his helpers.

"Listen, I'm sorry, come on down. It's important."

"It better be. In this line of work you have to do something to get paid," Jim said.

Jim walked across the roof like a mountain goat. Twenty-five years on a roof was a tough life. Tom though he'd held up well. He slid down the ladder at a steady rate of speed and stopped short, one step from the ground.

"I'm sorry about last night," Tom said.

"I hope you didn't call me down for that?" Jim said, as he lit a smoke.

"No, it's Jane's murder."

"You got somebody for it?"

"No, but maybe a suspect."

"Me again?"

"Knock it off, think about it. You knew her, I had to check it out."

"Look, what is it? I'm busy here," said Jim.

"Go to a meeting tonight. Maybe this Marco fits. Did he know Jane?"

"He had to. They were in the same group."

"You think he could have done it?" Tom asked.

"Tom, I don't know that many people there anymore. I never met any Marco," Jim said.

"How long did they say he was sober?" Tom persisted.

"I forget, about a year, yeah, a year."

"Jim, he disappears right after Jane goes missing. I don't like coincidences."

"There are no coincidences."

"What's that?"

"That's stupid wisdom I heard somewhere, it doesn't matter."

"Anyhow, he might be it. Do it for Jane," Tom said.

"I sure as shit ain't doing it for you."

"You'll do it?" Tom asked as Jim turned to go back up to the roof.

"Yes, I'll do it."

Tom watched Jim climb the ladder.

"Hey Jim! Just questions, no knuckles."

"Relax, I haven't hit anyone in two months."

Tom walked away to get in the car. Jesus, he hoped Jim didn't go bananas if he found the guy. This is how Tom got in trouble, using outside people. It was a tool he wasn't about to throw away. Jim was sober now. He would probably be okay. Tom knew Jim would go to the meetings, like he said, for Jane.

Tom killed the next two hours talking to Dan on his last day at the lab. He also had been up to see the Captain. He didn't think the Captain had really cared about a case for years. He was too busy figuring how to become Mayor.

Tom pulled up at the park. Eleven-forty. He lit a cigarette and got out of the car. He looked at the Jeep, six years he'd had it. He would miss it, but it would still be around. He'd tell Alice tomorrow that it was hers. He looked at his shoes as he paced back and forth. Back to the Jeep for a paper towel. He went around to the front of the Jeep and put his shoe on the bumper. He buffed his shoes, paced some more and smoked another cigarette.

Shelly was parked across the river in her Prowler. She faced the river and Tom. Her Bushnell binoculars were working great. She was laughing as she watched Tom. He looked like a husband outside of the delivery room. Nervous as a cat. She watched as he cleaned his shoes. He was so cute. Shelly knew that Tom didn't date much, or at all. Shelly thought in some ways she was older than Tom. A close personal relationship was definitely on the way.

Shelly would show mercy on Tom and be on time. He was like a little boy and she liked him for it. She laughed thinking of what his face would look like when she stepped out of the car.

Tom looked first one way, then the other. This time of day there were a lot of people coming and going to the park by the river. People, who worked at the local industrial park, jogged and walked around the river. It got crowded on a nice day. It was nice today.

Tom walked down to the river's edge. He looked at his watch; eleven fifty-five. He lit a cigarette and put a Tic Tac in his mouth. He was starting to sweat.

Tom heard a horn beep, turned and saw Shelly's car. He threw his smoke away, and started chewing his Tic Tac. He wondered if he smelled like smoke. For Pete's sake, he thought, I'm not going to kiss her.

Shelly stepped out of her car. She walked over to Tom, she thought he looked stunned. She was right, he was.

Tom watched Shelly walk across the parking lot to him. A car drove by with a couple teenagers hanging out the windows. One shouted, "I love you," to Shelly. Tom thought, that's my line. She stopped at the edge of the asphalt and waited. Tom felt he was climbing the grass slope in slow motion. Suddenly, he was in front of Shelly.

"Gee whiz, Shelly," Tom said.

"I'll take that as a compliment."

"Gee whiz, Shelly," Tom repeated.

"You said that already," she laughed.

"I mean wow! You look great."

"Shelly King, talent agent for Orion Pictures and the Mirage Casino in Las Vegas, my card, Sir."

"Hey, that's a good angle. A position of strength. I never would have guessed."

"I think the dancers will be willing to talk. They'll think their ship has come in."

"It's brilliant, Shelly," said Tom.

"I think so."

"Shelly, you look beautiful."

"Thanks, Tom. Do I look successful and filthy rich?"

"Is all that jewelry real?" Tom asked.

"Yes, but I usually only wear a piece at a time," Shelly said.

"Well you look Hollywood, that's for sure," Tom said.

"But do I look sexy, like a dancer who's made it big?"

"Shelly, when you walk in that club, I doubt anyone is going to be looking at the stage."

"Just the effect I was looking for."

"Gee Shelly, I don't feel so good about you going to a club looking like that."

"Afraid for me, Tom?"

"Well, yeah, I am."

"Tom, it's Shelly under all this gear. Remember me? The girl that kicked the butts of two guys that tried to take Dan's medical bag?"

"I know you did that and did it well, but I just can't put this picture together with that one."

"Tom, you're a riot," Shelly laughed.

Shelly wanted to push Tom's chin up to shut his mouth. It was hanging open. He didn't know where to look. She picked an outfit for maximum effect. Looking at Tom she knew she had picked well. Red high heels, a black mini skirt, real short, a red top you could look right through and a red mini bra underneath. She had her hair up very high and flashy, with a red highlight on one long piece hanging to one side. Definitely looked like Vegas. Gold rings, bracelets and chains. Flash, sexy and a little trashy. But Tom was lost in her face. He'd never seen her wear make-up. She knew she looked like a girl on the cover of Vogue. More importantly, Tom knew it, too.

"I guess you'll be okay. I mean it's the middle of the day, and all."

"Tom, you're really worried about me going to a club, aren't you?"

"Yes I am Shelly. I admit it."

Shelly walked over to Tom and put her arms around his waist.

"Tom, I'll be fine. I'm just going to check the two high tone joints on Route 130."

"I know you'll be okay, but heck, you're all legs and skin."

"Tom, you're the sweetest man in the world and one of the best looking."

Shelly lifted her head and kissed Tom, he kissed back.

"Tom, I'm going to check the girls out now," Shelly said, with her arms around Tom and his body against hers. I'll call you at four o'clock. Two hours per club should do it."

"Okay, Shelly," Tom said.

Shelly was laughing inside. She hadn't shaken anyone up like this, since she was dating in college. He was speechless, and she loved it. Tom White at a loss for words.

Shelly started to turn Tom loose. This was great. She wondered if she should help him to his car. He looked like he might need it. He looked lost.

"Tom, I'm going to go now."

"Okay, Shelly."

"Tom you should go right to your car. I think something's come up."

"What?" Tom asked.

Shelly pushed Tom away and slowly looked down below his belt.

Tom looked down, too.

"For Pete's sake, Shelly," Tom said.

Tom walked past Shelly, embarrassed and angry. His ears were as red as an apple. He got in his car.

"I'm sorry, Shelly," Tom said.

"I'm not, I'll call you around four. I guess you're younger than you thought."

Shelly walked to the Prowler laughing. He was so cute; he got his teeth bleached. She waved to Tom and burned rubber out the drive. She was happy. So, he *was* human.

Tom watched Shelly leave. He was embarrassed, but he had to laugh. There was no doubt about his feelings for her now. She had kissed him. He had known she was put together well, but, oh my. She reminded him of Ivana Trump, one of his favorite women. He often wondered why the Trump Man had left her. It couldn't have been her looks. Tom thought it probably wouldn't be right to ask Shelly to marry him on the first date. What a dope! He thought he'd better talk to Alice. She'd tell him how to handle what he was feeling. Tom only knew he was a goner with a boner.

Chapter Twenty

Wednesday Afternoon 3 p.m.

He was at his house, listening to the evening drivers come into the office at the cab company. He lived about three miles away. The audio was great. He'd long ago bugged the office. People who talked about him usually had car trouble, a lot of car trouble. One thing more than any other was important when driving cab. You had to be on time. No matter how good a driver you are, if you're not on time, you're gone.

He had bugged the office. It had been easy. He was the lone driver at night, eleven to seven. The day shift usually talked about him the most. Dan and Linda had both been fired last week. They were jealous, they'd wanted night shift. They thought they'd make more money at night. He fixed Dan's car by putting sand in the gas tank. He'd tried hard to get to work on time. But next, his ten-speed was stolen from behind his house. No . . . late four times in two weeks, he was fired.

Big mouth Linda was easy. She parked all night in a lot that was very dark. No windows in her apartment faced the lot. Her first day late, it was a flat. The next day, her belts had broken and the car overheated, late again. The third day, her oil pan had cracked. The oil was all over the lot. She was late again. The fourth day, she couldn't get her key to turn either lock on the doors. Four times late . . . she was gone.

He determined who kept their jobs. He was in charge. He knew the dispatcher was in the know, but Larry would never say anything. Larry had talked about Him a lot one morning, right after He had finished his shift. The next day, Larry was late. Larry never said anything more about Him. Larry knew when someone spoke poorly about Him, they would be late the next day. Larry had won money, betting people that someone would be late the next day. Then He thought Larry was getting greedy. Larry bet two hundred dollars that Stan would be late. He knew that Larry's betting would prove his suspicions. On this occasion, Larry lost. He didn't want anyone to be sure about anything, where He was concerned. He liked Larry to have suspicions, but certainly, no, never certainty.

He would control things. God needed His help and He was God's special person. Jerry had angered God. God's will would be done today. He didn't start his shift until eleven. If Jerry went to a meeting tonight, He'd help God with Jerry. He should have just enough time to get out to Voorhees, set the stage and get to work on time. He wouldn't see the results. But God wasn't really that interested in Jerry. God wouldn't need eye contact, for Jerry. God liked humble people. Jerry would be humbled, maybe killed. It was God's game, He'd decide. He still had trouble believing Jerry thought bullshit and lies the same.

He turned back to the paper. Dancer Slain No Apparent Motive! Well, he'd made the motive as plain as could be. They were bullshitting. He liked that.

Poor Marco, not even a mention. He couldn't blame the newspaper for that. Marco was too boring to rate a line. He was excited thinking that he determined some of what was news. All those people working for the paper. They did God's work, too. He was happy, happy enough, anyway.

He thought he'd park by the Federal Street Bridge tonight. He liked watching the cops at Jane's murder scene. He parked two city blocks away. The houses on those two blocks had been torn down in the early 70's. The view was wide open. A cab could hide in plain sight. He liked that. No one paid attention to a cab in the city. He watched the cops when they had found her body. They even went to Mag's mom's house. She had seen him take the girl into the house. He knew they'd think she was crazy. When he went with Mag to get the weeks supply of drugs, she called him El Diablo. He liked that, Mag was His friend, and Mag really liked Him. Sometimes, Mag told Him about people that God should be angry with. He'd asked God, if He was angry with these people. Most of the time, God said, "Yes, He was." He thought Mag was special, too. But Mag didn't know it and He wasn't telling him.

Oh well, Jerry tonight, then maybe He'd see if Bruce Jenner was looking for a cab. Brucey Baby was a riot. He had tried much harder than most; He'd like to give him service again. This time, He would have video. The camera He put in the trunk was working great.

The company had the business but He was a sub-contractor. He owned the cab He drove. They liked the setup. They didn't have to pay the insurance. They thought He was crazy. But they didn't know His friend Mag paid the insurance. Mag was a good friend.

He wondered if the striped bass were fighting over Marco's brains. It made a pretty picture.

Chapter Twenty-one

Wednesday, 4:30 p.m.

Tom had gone to talk to Alice. She laughed when Tom explained how he was feeling about Shelly. She told him to take it easy. Alice said all men thought like that before the first date. It was normal, she'd said.

Alice had done it again. She could see things more clearly than he could, when women were involved. Tom was still excited thinking about the date. He never felt like this about a woman. Dan had started this and he trusted Dan. It had to be right.

Dwayne had just left for home. He'd had no luck on the flowers. He also had checked Marco's house to see if he'd showed, yet. Jim had called the station with Marco's address, after calling Margie to get it. Tom knew he had lit a fire under Jim, and wasn't really comfortable with it, but he needed the help. Dwayne said the neighbors had told him no one had been in or out of Marco's. They said a guy had been staying there, but they hadn't seen him, either.

It was the fourth day since the murder. If something didn't turn up soon, he would start worrying that it wouldn't.

Willis and Ready were pulling into the parking lot.

Tom glanced at them; they weren't talking, which was unusual. He knew they had something. He knew it.

"I know you've got something," he greeted them.

"Damn! Here's the twenty," Willis passed a bill to Ready.

"How'd you know?" Willis asked.

"I just felt it," Tom said.

"White people are spooky," Willis said.

"I told you he'd know," Ready laughed.

"What is it?" Tom asked.

"I got it, Boss," Ready said.

"Good going Ready, I was betting on you turning something up. You're a regular blood hound," Tom said.

Ready glowed as he passed Tom a list.

"It's a short list," Tom said.

"Well Boss, it seems most people this time of year take the kids to the store to try the bike, first. Sales guy said if it had been before Christmas, the list would look like a telephone book," Ready informed him.

"Third name down looks real good," Willis said.

"Yes it does. Marco Campo," Tom said.

"The salesman at K Mart remembered him," Ready said.

"Any special reason?" Tom asked.

"Well, we asked him about men buying that model, men alone," Ready said, and then lit a smoke.

"Don't make me milk it out of ya," Tom yelled as he lit a cigarette.

"Okay, Tom, don't get red eared. Here it is," Ready said.

Willis cut in perfectly. Tom knew this would steam Ready and so did Willis. Tom smiled as he listened to Willis.

"The clerk remembered him because he was in a hurry. He had come to buy the bike in a cab. We were shown the paperwork, with the rebate slip. A twenty-dollar rebate, but Marco didn't want to wait for it. Clerk thought it was odd, but Marco did have a cab waiting. He signed the rebate slip with his name. But then he wouldn't wait for it. Clerk thought he was worried about the cab."

"Four days and we've got our man. It fits. I like him for it. He knew her, but what about the money?" Tom asked.

"The money?" Willis asked.

"Yeah, the money. I don't figure a guy just getting sober for having money to stage a murder," Tom said.

"Hell boss, he could have stolen it. He got sober, nobody said he got honest," Willis said.

"It looks damn good, I guess you're right. We're not looking at that much money. But the 'why', I'll get Jim to call some of those meeting people to see if he knew about the abortion, it could be that easy," Tom said.

"Yeah Tom, *Marco Campo* sounds Catholic to me, it might be that simple. "Maybe the Pope told him to do it," Willis said.

"Yeah, maybe the Pope told him to do it," Tom chuckled.

"Ready and Willis, here's Marco's address. Get over there and watch the house. If there is a rear entrance, cover it. If he shows up, cuff him," Tom said.

"I'm going to Judge Bisbing for a warrant, now drive," Tom said.

Tom took off for the Judge's chambers. He'd get the warrant. He thought about the suspect. Just sober a year, probably lonely, missing all the old people he used to drink with. Maybe Jane had worked her magic on him, too. She had plenty of charm. He could have had a crush on Sweet Jane, then learned of her abortion. Maybe he was a *Right to Life* nut, no. Could be some lady had aborted his baby. He liked the sound of that. Forget the Pope, Willis; this scenario was much more likely. He'd let Jane sit in for his lady. Oh yeah, he'd bet someone he'd known had an abortion. It felt good.

He hadn't heard from Shelly. He picked up his phone to call her. No, it was just after four. He'd wait. He realized he was still embarrassed. Gee whiz, he hadn't felt it coming. What an asshole! He cringed thinking about seeing her.

He slammed on his brakes just in time to get off the highway before the traffic circle. He better get Shelly off his brain. He would've been sitting in traffic for half an hour. He knew all the short cuts; now if he could keep his mind off Shelly's legs, everything would be cool.

Tom smiled again, thinking of Willis, stealing Ready's thunder. Ready was probably crying about that to Willis right now. Willis would enjoy that.

Chapter Twenty-two

Wednesday Evening Six p.m.

Tom stopped for burgers and cokes. Six o'clock. Willis and Ready would expect it. They had more than one thing in common. One thing was they had to eat every four hours. If they didn't eat regularly, they bitched and moaned as if it was life threatening. Tom didn't mind today. Today they'd earned it.

Shelly had called him to say one girl remembered Jane but no troubles could be recalled. The girls had gone crazy when they saw her. Shelly was surprised to find out that nearly half the dancers were gay. No wonder they didn't mind the work. They'd told her what a kick it was driving the men crazy, knowing full well that they weren't ever going to get anywhere. Shelly ended the call by telling Tom not to stand her up on Friday. If he did, a dancer named Nancy had said she'd be happy to take his place.

Tom wished he hadn't asked Shelly to go.

Tom pulled into Greenleaf Lane.

Willis was in the car, looking into a bag of Joyce's Donuts. Ready would be around back.

"You get any food?" Willis asked.

"Gee, I thought you were going to ask if I got the warrant, Willis."

"First things first, Lieutenant," Willis chuckled.

"Ready out back, Willis?"

"Oh, yeah."

"Let him stay there, let's check out the house."

Tom and Willis walked to the door. Willis looked through the window.

"Looks empty," he stated.

Tom drew his gun, "Willis, the door."

Willis dropped a shoulder about an inch and leaned. The door cracked then popped open and slammed the wall. The molding went with the door.

"Willis, you haven't lost your touch."

"No, Sir."

Tom stepped through the door. It was hot. An old air conditioner was in the window. He stepped to it and turned it on, working. He knew no one was here. Anybody would have had the air on. Tom holstered his gun.

The place was clean, if spartan. Tom waved Willis up the stairs. He looked through the small living room. The furniture was neat, but old. The floor was bare, but clean. Ashtrays had butts, but not many, all the same brand. He walked into the small kitchen. No microwave, no dishwasher, just an old range and a sink both clean and neat. Tom looked out the back door at Ready. He'd wait. He looked in the kitchen trash. Two cans of beans, one box of macaroni and cheese, and two empty packs of Newport. Tom didn't like it. A box of Ritz crackers and a few cans of tomato soup. That was the entire list of food in the house. Tom didn't like it. On the kitchen table was a large blue book and some AA pamphlets. A pad was on the table. The writing started . . . . "When I was a baby, my mom put paregoric on my gums." That was all that was written.

The refrigerator had a half-gallon of milk, still good, and two cans of Maxwell House Coffee, one opened.

The magnets on the refrigerator recommended, "*Easy Does It*" and "*keep it simple.*" Tom thought again, he didn't like it. There were some numbers under the magnets and a note that read "*remember to call people, don't isolate.*" The numbers were for Margie, Alan, Doug, Ron, Jennie and Jane.

That was something, but he still didn't like it.

Willis was coming down the stairs.

"Tom, this guy worked at the car wash on the circle, here's a pay stub. He didn't make enough to live on."

"I don't think this is our man."

"But the bike?" Willis reminded.

"Yeah, there's the bike, but I don't think so."

Willis had a seat. Tom did also.

"Should I bother going upstairs?"

"Tom, this guy ain't got shit. It's like he just moved in."

"Are there sheets on the bed?" Tom asked.

"Yeah, old ones, real old, but clean."

"Drawers?" Tom asked.

"About four dollars in pennies."

"Clothes, not many, about three changes I made it," said Willis.

"Bathroom?"

"Soap, one towel, one Playboy and a little dirty laundry."

"Well Willis, it looks like the roommate got the TV. The cables still hanging and here's the bill."

"Nice guy," Willis said.

"Yeah."

"You don't like him for it, do you?"

"This kid was starving, he didn't set up that basement," Tom said.

"You don't know that, you just feel it," Willis said.

"That's right, I just feel it."

"Now what?" asked Willis.

"Now I get someone over here to take prints and fibers and the rest. If her prints are here, I'll feel a lot better. Get on the phone to the crime lab. I'll get an all points out for this guy. Hand me that picture," Tom said.

"This one?" Willis handed it to Tom.

"Looks like it's recent. I'll let Jim look at it. Probably an AA group, the sign says *Spiritual Retreat*."

"*Spiritual Retreat, the Pope*, I still like that angle." Willis said.

"Yeah the Pope. Sure Willis."

"What about Ready?"

"I've got food in the car, tell Ready to get it and you both hang here until the lab is done. Then get someone just coming on duty to hang out in here. But I don't think this guy's coming back."

"Another feeling?" Willis asked.

"I'm out of here, is that air working?" asked Tom.

"It's trying, see you tomorrow Tom."

"Your kid got practice tonight?"

"He does, Tom," Willis smiled.

"All right, as soon as the unit comes, you can take off. Don't tell Ready where you're going, just tell him I want you somewhere else."

"Don't worry, I won't."

"Tomorrow, Willis."

"Thanks Tom, you're okay for a white guy."

Tom wasn't feeling good. Marco could be the player, but it would be unlikely. This kid's got three cans of soup and he's buying a bike to leave for effect. Tom didn't like it.

Chapter Twenty-three

Wednesday Night 9 PM

Tom was supposed to be at Dan's now, to pick up the Lincoln. He'd call Dan. He pictured Shelly on the phone telling Dan about his condition this afternoon. He hoped not, for Pete's sake. If Dan knew, Tom would know right away. Dan couldn't keep a straight face. Tom called him and Dan said there was no hurry. He had slept late for the first time in a long time and he'd be up late.

Tom thought he'd go look in on Sugar. He pulled into Our Lady of Lourdes Hospital. Spots were tight, but there was a cab pulling out of the lot. He waited for the spot, but the guy seemed to be having trouble with the car. Screw it, he drove out of the lot and made a U-turn, then parked on the street. As he walked up the stairs to the hospital, he noticed that the cab had made it out of the spot. Tom thought he should have waited the extra fifteen seconds. He was edgy. The case was a mess. If this Marco was the culprit, he'd eat his hat.

Sugar was on the bed asleep. Tom looked around the room. Flowers, a couple of cards from the station, magazines. He thought someone was taking good care of Sug. Cup cake wrappers were everywhere.

Tom turned to leave; he'd stop in tomorrow.

"I'm awake, where you going?" Sugar asked.

"I thought you were asleep, I was going to come back."

"I dose off, but I can't get any real rest. This bed doesn't go flat, the nurses say it does. But it doesn't, it's broken and I want a new bed."

"I'll tell the doctor to get you a new bed."

"You better go to the golf course then, I haven't seen any doctors around here. Hospital food's not for me. Before you go, get me a chocolate shake from the snack bar, okay?"

"Okay, Sugar. You must be feeling better. They say when you start bitching, you're getting better," said Tom.

"Then I must be ready to be discharged, I've been bitching all day."

"How's the gut?"

"Shit, it's nothing."

"Painful?"

"Damn right, where's my damn pill?"

A nurse walked in the room. A little thing, she didn't look eighteen.

"Here's your pill Officer Carter, right on time, as usual," the nurse said.

"If it was on time, my stomach wouldn't hurt. Maybe I'm supposed to get eight pills a day and you nurses are keeping two for a party," Sugar said.

"You bet we are. We're having a party downstairs right now. Who's your friend?"

"That's Lieutenant White, he's going to see that you get me a new bed."

"He's cute, is he single?"

"He's single, single as a man can get. I tried to get him a date, but he ain't interested."

"You gay, Lieutenant?" the nurse asked.

"No, I'm not gay," Tom glared at Sugar.

"That's good, the name's Nancy Yablonski, call me anytime."

"I'll remember that. How old are you?"

"You can't ask a woman that."

"You can't be ashamed of your age, yet?"

"No, everyone asks me that question for the opposite reason. I guess they don't think I'm old enough to be a nurse."

"Are you? I don't mean to be rude."

"Yes I am, I'm twenty-two. Legal age, how about that date?"

"I've got a date, just got together with a girl."

"He's lying, show him something. He'll come around." Sugar laughed.

"I'll take his word for it, Officer Carter. You try and get some rest. A couple big guys are coming up from the first floor to get you into a new bed. Be about an hour."

"It's about time!" Sugar said.

"Nice meeting you." The nurse left.

"Jesus, Sugar, I can get my own women."

"Since when?"

"It is a little tough for me, I don't drag them off the boulevard."

"Some damn nice girls work for a living there."

"If you say so."

"I do."

"Dan's done, he retired," said Tom, hoping to change the subject.

"Well good for him, it's about time. Shelly must be sick about it. Shelly! I bet you're going out with Shelly. That's it, the ears are going red. Ha, ha, ha, well it's about time." Sugar laughed.

"I'll go get your shake," Tom said.

"Ha, ha, ha, Tom and Shelly," Sugar said, as Tom went for his shake.

For Pete's sake, He must have been the last person to find out Shelly liked him. He wondered if everyone knew he'd thought about her. They had to, they were cops. Tom felt the blood rush to his ears. Maybe a doctor could do something about red ears. He doubted it.

Tom had taken the shake back to Sugar and said his good-byes. Sugar had asked for film of the first date. Typical of him. Everyone was getting a kick out of this. So why wasn't he?

Tom went to his car. There was a slip of paper under the wiper, it read, "Jane was a liar."

Tom spun around looking for someone, anyone, a man, he ran to the corner. No one! He walked back to the lobby. The security guard was there.

"Did you see anyone at that car?"

"What car?"

"The cop car!"

"I didn't see anybody."

"Are you front door security?"

"Yes, I am."

"Then I recommend you get off your ass and start doing your job."

"But I watch the lobby."

"Yeah, yeah, yeah," Tom said.

Tom walked back to the car. He took the note and folded it into his top pocket. This was going to the lab. He knew Jane's killer left the note. Tom could feel it. Son of a bitch, he wasn't in there more than a half-hour. How did the killer know Tom was there? Only Dan knew where Tom was going.

"The creep must have seen me at the crime scene," Tom thought aloud. He must have still been around. The scum must have hung around for kicks. Tom was angry, but he was relieved at the same time. Leaving the note was risky. Risk takers get caught. But would it be soon enough or would he watch another body being picked up? Was he following me, Tom wondered? He checked his weapon; follow me, please.

Tom was at Dan's. No one had followed him, he was sure of it. Why had he come here, to visit? The car! He was rattled; he'd been on this force a long time. He'd laughed at movies that showed the killer screwing with a cop. It didn't really happen, but it had.

Tom saw Dan through the french doors of the living room. There had been many good times here. But right now, Tom couldn't remember any. He walked up to the door and tried it. The door opened. Tom would talk to Dan about the unlocked door, but didn't want to alarm him.

"Hey Dan, it's Tom."

"Come in. I thought I locked that door. I should be more careful."

"Yes, you should Dan, you never know."

"Don't tell Shelly or she'll camp out here until I go to Israel."

"I wanted to talk to you about Shelly, maybe later. Something else has come up."

"You don't look good Tom, sit down!"

"I'm okay. I do my best thinking on my feet."

"What's up, Doc?" Dan asked.

"When I left the hospital tonight, there was a note under the wiper."

"Anyone we know leave it?" asked Dan.

"No."

"The killer?" Dan asked.

"I think so."

"What did it say?"

"'Jane was a liar', that's all, just 'Jane was a liar.'"

Tom took a seat and lit a smoke. Dan reached for his pipe.

"Beer, Tom?"

"Oh, yeah. Bring the six pack."

Tom felt better after telling Dan. Funny, he thought, but true, that saying about a burden shared. Nothing had been accomplished, but he felt relieved. Dan walked back in the room with two huge cans of Foster's Beer.

"It's not a six pack, but it's got to be half a six."

"Perfect," Tom said as he took the cold can.

"You know, he must have seen you at the scene."

"I know."

"You'd know if you were being followed," said Dan.

"I can't tell you *yes* with any honesty, that I would have."

"You can't?"

"No, I can't. I've been out to lunch most of the week," Tom said.

"What's on your mind? No! I think I know."

"You're right, Dan, I think I'm in love with Shelly."

"I've known that since the accident."

"What's that?"

"You two visited me every day for hours. And don't take this wrongly. You two were together, and both so happy. Neither of you was there to see me. You were both there to be together. It was so obvious. I thought you'd be dating in days."

"Hey Dan, that's not fair. We care for you a lot. Heck, we love you."

"I know that, but lean back in your chair for one minute, one full minute, remember those weeks. Then tell me I'm wrong. No, I mean it. One minute, by my watch. If you tell me I'm wrong, I'll apologize."

"All right, say when Dan."

"When."

"Tom leaned back in the chair. He thought about Dan's visits. What did he remember, it was two years ago. What did he feel then, excitement and expectation. Tom didn't need the remaining minute. In his gut, he knew Dan was right. Tom looked at Dan. He was smiling at Tom.

"Well, Tom?"

"You're the doctor, and I'm embarrassed to say, you're at least 80% right."

"That's fair. I guess I did get 20% of your attention. And I'd grade Shelly about the same."

"Dan, I'm sorry."

"There you go again, we're too close for that stuff. We are the way we are. How you and Shelly feel about each other is as natural as the seasons. I rather enjoyed the show, but I was surprised neither of you caught it."

"Am I that dense?" Tom asked.

"The forest for the trees, it happens more than you think."

"The older I get, the dumber I think I'm becoming."

"You're as sharp as a tack, Tom. Love just hasn't been your game. Let's consider this a rookie season."

"Love! Yeah, I guess I am a rookie," Tom said.

"But let's switch horses, now that we have firmer footing. Can you think of anyone out of place at the scene?"

"I've tried, but I come up blank. There were a few old folks around, a couple stray kids, and two crack heads in an abandoned house that Clark yelled at. But nobody that could be our man."

"That's good Tom. Someone else was watching, though. He had to be watching, he recognized you."

"But I checked that area close."

"Umm." Dan leaned back and drew on his pipe.

"Dan, why do I have the feeling you're waiting for me to say what I'm going to say?"

"Say it, Tom."

"I looked too close. He might have been blocks away, or he could have been a mile away on a building."

"That's right, he may have been, but I don't think so."

"What else is there?"

"He knew he would be seen, or rather he knew you'd see him, but not see him."

"I don't follow. Unless you're saying it was a cop?"

"Tom, no cop did this. After all, money was spent."

"Hey! That's right." They both laughed.

"No Tom, this type of personality is like the firebug caught at the fire. They want to see it. They want to be a part of it."

"Maybe it was the old lady across the street."

"Sleep on it Tom, I bet it will hit you like a hammer."

"Sounds good to me, Dan, but I really don't think I missed anything."

"Maybe we're both wrong, but I doubt it."

Tom leaned back and looked at the once gracious living room. It was stark, with just an old sofa, and Dan's old recliner.

"When you sell your stuff Dan, you don't fool around. I'm surprised you kept the sofa and recliner," said Tom.

"I couldn't even pay them to take the sofa, it weighs a ton, it's a bed. The recliner goes to Tel Aviv."

"You're joking, it's thirty years old."

"It fits my old bones. I'm shipping it. Shelly was surprised, too."

"For shipping costs, you could buy new."

"*You* buy new, it goes."

"Like the chair Frazier's dad has on the show."

"Who's Frazier?" asked Dan.

"I forgot, you're a reader. Frazier's a guy on a sitcom."

"Is *sitcom* a word, I really dislike it. I don't accept it as a word."

"It probably isn't, Dan. I won't accept it either. Anymore beer?"

"You're driving."

"I'll sleep on the sofa. Who's going to miss me?"

"Right you are. Two beers coming up. Hey Tom, I'll bet you can't say that this time next year."

"What's that, Dan?"

"Who's going to miss me."

The Foster's was doing its work. Tom was feeling relaxed. He knew he would just be spinning his wheels if he kept after it now. He'd sleep on it, like Dan said. Tom straightened up; he was sober as a judge.

"Dan, hey Dan, where are you?" he yelled.

"I'm out here, be quiet."

Tom stepped out the french doors into the back yard.

"What are you doing?" Tom whispered.

"I'm watering the roses."

"Oh, I'm sorry. Dan, do you think he saw Shelly?"

"Call her."

Tom went to the phone. He punched the numbers.

"Hello."

"Hello Shelly," Tom said.

Hi Tom, what's up?"

Tom heard some laughter.

"You alone? Oh, I get it, what's up?"

Tom heard more laughter.

"I'm sorry Tom, I know you're easily embarrassed. Why did you call?" asked Shelly.

"Hold on a second," Tom said.

Dan was speaking to Tom. "Tell her we are test driving the Lincoln because I'm giving it to you. You want her opinion."

"Jesus Dan, that's lame."

"Try it."

"Shelly, Dan's giving me the Lincoln and he wants you to be there for his last ride," said Tom.

"What? Tell him he can stop playing Cupid."

"Hold on Shelly."

"Dan, I'm telling her."

"I guess you have to. Do it."

"Shelly look. Don't get scared."

"Are you two drunk?"

"Shelly, please listen. Get your gun and wait for us. We'll be right over. We're serious. The killer left a note. He's playing games. You could be one of the players."

"I've got my gun in my hand now."

"Really?"

"Tom, I know you aren't a practical joker . . . really."

"We'll be there in ten minutes."

"Tom, I'll be alright."

"We're on our way." Tom hung up.

"Ready Dan?"

"I'm ready."

Dan locked the door, and they walked to Tom's Jeep. The Lincoln was in the garage. They pulled out fast.

"We should have thought of this sooner," Tom said.

"Relax Tom, Shelly's not a victim."

"I know, I know, but you know!"

"Yes, I do, you worry about the ones you love."

"Right, damn right," said Tom.

Chapter Twenty-four

Wednesday Night 11 PM (Killer just starting his shift)

He was pulling into his regular spot at the High Speed Line. He got out of the cab, opened the trunk to get cleaning supplies. He wanted to clean the car and turn the camera on. As he was washing the windows he was excited thinking about the camera. He knew he'd get some good footage. He was really feeling great. He'd stopped by the hospital to make sure Jerry had gone to the AA meeting in the cafeteria. Jerry was there in his biker costume. He knew one of the bikes out back was his, but he couldn't tell one bike from another. They all looked alike to him. What a bonus he'd gotten. Film of the cop on Jane's case waiting for his parking spot. Film, of the cop. The cop, looking angry, confused, impatient, he felt he was the reason for everything in the cop's head. He knew he was. It was God's will, he knew that also. It had been such a rush. He had gone around the block and left the note. This was great. He felt so in charge, so important. All the while setting up Jerry. He knew it was God's way of telling him how well he was doing, His work.

Jerry would be leaving the diner, right about now, he guessed. In the development where Jerry lived, there was a sharp curve about a quarter mile before Jerry's house. He had seen Jerry ride. He rode fast. He knew Jerry would be flying when he hit the curve. He parked on the curve, it was just after dark. He took a five-gallon jug of vegetable oil mixed with Skin-so-soft, a very slippery combination. He poured it on the section of the curve where Jerry would need to brake. It should work like a dream. He'd had to take off his shoes to drive to the cabstand. His feet were so slippery he couldn't keep them on the pedals. He was cleaning his shoes and pedals now. He was trying not to laugh, but it was so funny. He was cleaning up; Jerry was messing up, oh, what a great day.

There were three cabs at the Speed Line. He would have to wait a while to screw around with a customer. He heard the train coming. The people came down the stairs. A good-looking girl was walking to his cab, he'd take her. She didn't look like she was in a hurry. While he was driving his fare home his thoughts turned to the cop. He knew he had to screw with that cop again. He couldn't wait to get home and view the film. He was a genius; the camera was such a good idea. He only turned it on to test it, and then the cop pulled up behind him. Definitely God's will. There were no coincidences. He doubted Jerry would be in the paper but he'd check. Great ideas were rushing into his head, he was finally happy.

Chapter Twenty-five

Wednesday Night 11 PM (Tom and Dan at Shelly's)

Jim had gone to the meeting. He regretted going. But shit, it was great. A kid about eighteen was doing all the talking. The people that had been around awhile, all knew he was on a pink cloud. He was just happy to be alive and sober.

Jim remembered his first ninety days sober. He'd felt pretty much like the kid. He loved everybody back then. But like Jim told Tom, he was a magnet for screwed up people. Jim met a girl in AA; well, he met lots of girls. But this one girl loved him something terrible. Unfortunately, his head was all screwed up and he didn't appreciate her. She was a good woman. He had wrecked that romance. The girl always wore spandex. He didn't like spandex, but five years later he still thought about her a lot. He hoped she was happy. He also hoped she didn't come to a meeting with some asshole on her arm. At least not while he was there.

He hadn't found out where Marco was. Everyone was bumming about Jane. So was he. But this was the last meeting he was going to. He wasn't going to be there, if the Spandex lady walked in. He couldn't take that. She'd finally told him to leave her alone, after he broke her heart once too often. He'd never get married. It was crazy but every time he went into a store or to a movie, he thought maybe he'd bump into her and get another chance. But, no luck. If she saw him at a meeting, she might think he was looking for her. He had his pride and his anger and his loneliness. He worked hard for all three and he thought he got what he deserved.

Between Jane getting murdered, and the girl, he couldn't stay any longer. AA wasn't fucked up, he was. All he had was one good dog, one good friend,

Patty, and one hell of a gambling problem. Yet, he thought about the girl that wore spandex. He thought he'd get drunk tonight. It had been a long time. Yeah, six beers and kick the shit out of some loud mouth. Sounds like a winner. He sure missed that girl.

If Tom wanted any more information, he'd have to quit drinking, declare himself an alcoholic and go himself.

He should get drunk and hit that son of a bitch. "Alibi! I had to give him an alibi." He'd tell Tom he didn't have shit and he could go to hell. He'd made Jim remember that girl, the one he still loved, but would probably never see again. Seeing all her old friends was really depressing. Yeah, he'd get drunk. What the hell, he had bail money. He thought getting drunk would close the door on AA and the girl in spandex, forever. It sounded like a damn good idea.

Oh, the hell with it. He'd probably get a D.W.I. and be out of business. Roulette was pretty much like getting drunk. The wheel spins around and you don't have any idea where it will stop. He'd keep his license and go play roulette. Maybe he'd get drunk tomorrow, but not today. He'd take that girl back if she was blind and weighed three hundred pounds. He thought he was beginning to understand what love was. Too bad it was too late. Tom can go to hell.

Tom and Dan pulled into Shelly's driveway. Her car was there. As they walked to the front door, the light went on.

"Come on in. It didn't take you long."

Dan gave Shelly a hug and walked up the stairs of her split-level to the living room. Tom walked over and gave her a hard squeeze.

"Tom, you're shaking," Shelly said.

"I'll be okay."

Shelly looked into his eyes and squeezed his hand hard. She thought he was going to cry. She knew she was.

"Go up with Dan, I'll be right with you," she said.

"Well Tom, thank God for that."

"You said it! I want her to go away for a while, it just makes sense."

"I understand what you're saying, but I wouldn't put it to her like that," Dan said.

"Shelly doesn't run, it's not in her."

"There's no chance?"

"None, if she feels about you like I think she does, she's going nowhere."

Shelly came up the stairs. She was holding a picture. The picture was a woman in fifties clothes. The expression was hard to put into words. Shelly had handed it to Tom.

"It's an amazing picture, isn't it?" she asked.

"I couldn't describe this woman, her smile is something . . . like Mona Lisa.

"That was my Grandmother. She survived the Nazis, I'll survive this case," Shelly said.

Shelly wasn't done talking. They both knew that. She was pacing now. She had taken the picture from Tom. She looked at it, kissed it and passed it to Dan. He held it with reverence, reminded Tom of a Rabbi with a Torah. Shelly sat down next to Dan.

"Tom, that woman raised me when my mother died. She lived here in this house. She was as kind, intelligent, and loving as they come. She was also about one thousand years old in experience. As she put it, the experience of a life of joy and suffering."

"That's what I couldn't explain. The picture shows you both, at once. It's amazing," said Tom.

"I hoped you'd see it."

"Tom, she told me many good things, and a lot of bad."

"She was wonderful Tom, I knew her well," Dan said.

"She knew a man that loved her once. But in her day, the woman had to wait for him to speak. She made me promise not to make that mistake."

"What do you mean, Shelly?" Tom said.

"Do you love me, Tom?"

"Yes, I think I have since the accident Dan had." Tom stunned himself.

"I love you, Tom. We're getting married before Dan goes to Israel. He's all I have left of a family. He's my whole family, not blood, but no less family. My Grandmother could have asked that man if he loved her. But she didn't. He was sent to Auschwitz. If she had spoken, they would have had two years together before the Nazis deported everyone East. She regretted that until the day she died. I'll not have those regrets. We will get married next week. I made other promises, and I wouldn't love you if I wasn't sure you'd respect them. One was we'd never go to bed angry. Another was the children will be raised as Jews."

"I'll marry you, Shelly. If we have children, I'd be proud if they were raised as Jews. We're still about six million short in this crazy world." Tom said.

"Good, I'll call the Rabbi tomorrow."

"What a woman, eh Tom!" Dan jumped up with Shelly and did a dance.

"Tom, you can dance with us," Shelly said.

"I guess I'll need a crash course in dancing. I've never danced," Tom said.

"Dance at the wedding. Shelly, my leg's killing me. Let's have wine to celebrate," Dan said.

"Wine, we'll have champagne!" Shelly ran to the kitchen.

Dan walked over and hugged Tom. "I'm so happy for all of us."

"I can't believe it, but it's wonderful," Tom said.

"Tom you know, in a lot of ways, she's as old or older than you are. It's a good match," Dan smiled.

"I guess I'll get used to people thinking she's my daughter."

"That's a problem every man should have," Dan was laughing.

Shelly carried a nice silver tray downstairs. She hadn't just thrown it together. Cheese, some bread and chilled champagne.

"Pretty sure of yourself Shelly," Dan smiled.

"Pretty sure," she laughed, setting down the tray and threw her arms around Tom and kissed him.

"Are you happy, Tom? I am."

Tom couldn't say anything. He just held her. His eyes said volumes.

"He's happy already. Let's toast! To the happy couple, may they live a long life and have many children," Dan toasted.

"I think about five will do it," Shelly said as she picked up her glass.

"Shelly, five kids will be expensive," Tom smiled. "I'm not rich."

"Good thing I am," she grabbed Tom and pulled him onto the sofa.

"Shelly, call me tomorrow morning and we'll go to the Rabbi," Dan said. "Tom give me your keys."

"Where are you going?" Tom asked.

"I'm not so old I don't know when to leave two people in love."

Shelly walked over to the table and threw Dan the keys.

"Call you tomorrow. Dan, thank you," she said.

"Dan, what about the killer?" Tom said.

"That's your job. I'm retired. You're going to solve this case. He made a mistake, he'll make more."

"Goodnight, Dan." She kissed the old man at the door.

"Goodnight, Precious."

Shelly walked over to the sofa and put her Grandmother's picture on the table. She looked at it.

"She was so smart."

"So's her granddaughter."

"As soon as you solve this case, we'll take a long honeymoon."

"I don't know if I can get the time that fast, Shelly."

"Oh, so now you've got the case solved."

"You heard Dan. He's usually right."

"He is, isn't he?" Shelly smiled.

"I hope he is this time," said Tom.

"Have you ever seen Israel?"

"No, but I have a feeling that I'm going to."

"Tom, we'll get along fine."

Shelly dropped next to Tom on the sofa. Tom put his arms around her sleek and solid body.

"Shelly, the killer must have seen me at the scene."

"Are you still worried about me?"

"Yes."

"I know you are and I love that about you, but Tommy, if he comes around here, I'll drop him like a bad habit."

"How can you be so tough, and beautiful at the same time?"

"I'm my Grandmother's child."

"I guess that's a pretty good answer."

"Tom, are you angry at me?"

"No, why?"

"I wanted to be certain I didn't break a promise. Let's go to bed."

Chapter Twenty-six

Thursday morning 7 AM

Tom had called Dwayne early. They wouldn't meet at the park by Cooper River today or for a while. Maybe Jane's killer had seen them there. Tom wanted to meet somewhere that would make it difficult for anyone to watch them, without being spotted.

They decided to meet at a diner across from the Courier Post Building. They'd stay in the back of the lot. No river view, but very private. Tom had asked Shelly to come with him and spend the day with Doris and her father. She'd laughed at Tom, but she knew he worried about her and she liked that.

Tom told Shelly she wouldn't be bored. Big Daddy would keep them company. Tom was happy he was visiting. Shelly would be safe, he knew that. Until this guy was caught, he'd try his best to keep her in someone's company. A tougher job he couldn't imagine. She was very independent. She hadn't blinked when he suggested she go to the strip clubs. She had guts, maybe too many. He wasn't worried, and he didn't want to seem like a male chauvinist, but his heart was in charge now, everyone with any sense knows that when the head and heart collide in man, the heart wins that contest.

They had a beautiful night. Tom thought he was dreaming. He woke up. He'd opened his eyes and she was there. They'd made love and it *was* love, in the true sense. She was a woman and she would be faithful to everyone she knew. To Dan, her Grandmother, her synagogue, her faith, her friends and he was sure, himself.

As Tom pulled up to the building, Dwayne was running to the car.

"Shelly, have fun today. I'll say goodbye now. It looks like we're in a hurry," Tom said.

"I always have fun, you be careful. Give me a kiss."

Tom kissed her and she jumped out of the car.

"Where's the fire, Dwayne?" Shelly asked.

"National Park," Dwayne said as he climbed in the car.

Tom wheeled out of the lot, past the river and flipped on the siren. A quick left and they were headed south on Route 130.

"Why are we going to National Park, Dwayne?" Tom asked.

"I just had a call. They've found Marco Campo."

"Found?"

"Yeah, floating in two feet of water. Some tourists at the Battlefield spotted the body."

"That'll make their whole trip."

"Tom, could be he jumped off the bridge, suicide."

"No way Dwayne, whoever killed Jane Comfort, had no conscience. Her killer didn't commit suicide."

"Maybe, maybe not, everybody feels guilty sometimes."

"Not this sociopath. If anything, he's feeling better than ever. We'll know when we see the body if he's a jumper."

They drove the five miles down Route 130 in silence. Tom turned into National Park and headed for the river.

"Willis and Ready will be looking for us at the diner," Tom said.

"*In* the diner, by now," Dwayne said.

"I should have had my coffee," Tom said.

"No coffee Tom, and your talking? Amazing."

"I feel good this morning."

"Did I see Shelly kiss you goodbye?"

"I guess you did."

"Warming up for tomorrow's date?"

"Yeah, I guess we are."

"Look over there!" Dwayne pointed down a lane that led to the river. The lights from an ambulance flashed up the lane. There were a few cops there; it had to be the body.

"That's it, good eyes."

Tom pulled down the lane. Rusty Sheets, the National Park cop he knew, was there.

"Yo, Rusty. Where is he?"

"Hi Tom, he's where he washed up. Nobody's around and we thought we'd let you see him first."

"Good thinking Rusty. You ever want a good job in the city, let me know."

"Gee thanks Tom, but I like it here."

"Smart and common sense, too. No Rusty, you'd never be happy in Camden."

"Hi Dwayne, what are you doing with Tom. Working your way back down the ranks?" Rusty said.

"Trying not to, Rusty," Dwayne said.

"Rusty, just take us to Marco, okay?" Tom said.

"Yes sir, Lieutenant, this way please."

They followed Rusty through some brush and down a rocky slope to the beach. The body was floating face up.

"Jesus Tom, he's purple," said Dwayne.

"Floaters swell up, they always look like that while they're in the water, the first couple days anyway."

"All right, Rusty, you've got the boots on, bring him out," Tom said.

Rusty waded into the water. There was a commotion in the water, a large fish rushed away from the body.

"Striper! They love anything bloody," Rusty said.

"Jesus, what's that?" Dwayne said.

"What's left of his brains," Rusty said.

"Shut up guys, let me look him over. No humor Rusty, I haven't eaten yet."

"Okay Tom, I wasn't trying to be funny," Rusty laughed.

Tom bent down next to the body on the beach. He rolled the body over.

"Still think he jumped?" Tom asked.

"He's no jumper, Tom," Dwayne said.

"That's right, someone smashed his head in."

"Tom! It's empty, his head," Dwayne gasped.

"Stripers are running. I guess they thought those brains were blood worms." Rusty laughed again.

"You're so funny you should go on stage," Tom said.

"Dwayne, look at this wound."

"Jesus Tom, the back of his head is gone."

"This guy didn't jump, he was dumped."

"Rusty, he's all yours."

"What do you mean? He was wanted in Camden. Your people should take him."

"No Rusty, only alive was he wanted. This job is for the Gloucester County Coroner. We've no interest in his corpse. Good luck. See you later. If he finds anything unusual have him give us a call," said Tom.

"Tom, come on. The City's better equipped than we are. Help me out here," Rusty said.

"No can do, City policy. Have a nice day Rusty. Let's go Dwayne."

"Yeah, good for you. Next time we'll wait till the tide's coming in and we'll send 'em back to ya," Rusty said.

Tom and Dwayne walked to the car. Dwayne was looking pale.

"Dwayne, you okay?" Tom asked.

"I can't get that fish swimming away from him, out of my mind."

"Sickening, I know."

"I've never seen anything eating brains before. Give me a little air will you?"

It was early in the day. Tom didn't like air conditioning.

"We'll have plenty of air when we get moving," Tom said.

Tom knew Dwayne would come around soon. Most cops didn't stay upset long. He lit up a cigarette.

"Do you have to smoke?"

"It helps me think. The windows are open."

"Tom, let's get some coffee."

"You bet, up at Dunkin Donuts."

Tom was keeping an eye on Dwayne, he was shaking it off.

"He was murdered. You don't land on the back of your head if you jump from a height," Tom said.

"I tend to agree. No other marks on the body. Someone came up behind him with a weapon, a heavy weapon."

"You know what I think, Dwayne?"

"No I don't. Maybe I should, but I'm still a little green."

"Can't blame you. I think the killer had Marco buy the bike."

"Murdered him to shut him up?"

"Could be," Tom said.

"Where are we now, nowhere."

"I wouldn't say that. These two knew each other from AA."

"Tom, I'm no drinker but their have to be hundreds of people that go to AA meetings in town every week."

"Maybe more than a thousand, Dwayne, but I think our killer is one of that number."

"Tom most of those people are really nice."

"Most cops are nice, too. But I can think of a couple bad apples."

"I'm sending them home today. I want them on night shift; starting tomorrow night, us, too."

"Willis and Ready? So what about today?" Dwayne said.

"Let's go to the river, hit some balls and talk. Maybe we've got something we don't know we have," Tom said.

"If we do, it sure is laying low."

"Laying low makes me think of that girl in the basement."

"Thanks Tom, now when I hear those words, that's what I'll think of."

"Being a cop's great isn't it? I've got a hundred sayings in my head that effect me the same way."

Let's change the subject. I wonder what the girls are up to?" Dwayne said.

"*The girls*, sounds good doesn't it?"

"You and Shelly seem to be hitting it off," Dwayne chuckled.

"You could say that," Tom smiled.

"What aren't you telling me?"

"I'm just in a good mood."

"Okay, you don't want to talk about it. That's alright with me," Dwayne said.

"Dwayne, we haven't had our first date yet, what could there be to tell? That's if I was the kind of guy that told. Which I'm not."

"Knock it off Tom. I know something's up. I notice unusual behavior. You were wound up this morning, and before the coffee."

"I've been exercising. I've been feeling better in the mornings."

"Okay, so you're not talking."

"Not about Shelly, maybe Doris can fill you in later. Some things are up to the woman to make known."

"Jesus, she's pregnant?"

"She's not pregnant."

"No chance?" Dwayne asked.

"I'm not talking about this subject anymore. All right?"

"You dog!" Dwayne laughed.

"Look, drop it, you're way off track. That's all I'm telling you."

"That's all you've got to say. Doris will have the whole scoop, anyway. No one can keep a secret from Doris. People just have to tell her their secrets. Yeah, Doris will have the scoop."

"There is no scoop. Look I'll flip you this coin, loser pays for the balls," Tom said.

Tom and Dwayne walked into the driving range.

"Heads or tails, Dwayne?"

"Heads."

Tom flipped the coin up and let it fall to the ground.

"Tails! All right!" Tom shouted.

"Shit, how much are baskets here?"

"Six bucks apiece for medium."

"Good Lord, Tom, we've got to get one of these places. I'm serious. Look out there."

Tom looked at the range. About fifty men and women were steadily knocking balls out, over and into the water. It was only early morning and this place was half full.

"Damn gold mine, isn't it?"

"Absolutely, but what is it? It's about five acres of land, some concrete tees, some fence, a mower or two, and an old tractor to collect the balls. No greens to keep up. No fairways to groom. This place is selling time. Tom, time is free. They use the same balls over and over."

"Snack bar's probably raking it in, too," Tom said.

"Ice cream itself has to be paying the freight here."

"You might be onto something, Dwayne, but you need the land."

"Tom, I've got ten acres."

"Where?"

"Mississippi."

"Lots of businesses that do great around Jersey die elsewhere," Tom warned.

"I know that Tom, but I could sell that land and use the money to buy around here somewhere."

"Are you talking seriously?"

"I am, Tom. Let's do it. You must have something put away, you're single."

"My house is paid for, but that's about it. I spread it around when I have it. Dan thinks I should stop helping people out so much."

"What's the house worth?"

"About one seventy-five, I bought it at the right time. It's tripled in value since I made my first payment."

"That could be your half," Dwayne smiled.

"Great, where am I going to live?"

"Shelly's?" Dwayne asked.

"We'll talk about it later. It's such a standard cop conversation, it's aggravating me."

Dwayne teed up his golf ball and hooked the ball out of bounds.

"Yeah Tom, I can hit the ball two fifty every time, but where it goes is out of my hands."

"Keep your head down, your mechanics are good."

Tom's balls were falling fifty to ten feet around a flag, without exception.

"Tom, if you can put the ball down on the green every drive, why don't you golf?"

"For one simple reason, Dwayne. I can't putt to save my life. Just can't read a green. I refuse to play eighteen anymore. I can't afford the clubs I throw in the water."

"Can't putt at all?"

"If I'm ten feet from the hole, I can get down in three."

"Oh, you really can't putt."

"I just told you that."

"I know, but something that awful takes a while to sink in," Dwayne laughed.

"Tom, if cops are so happy being cops, why are we always talking about some other way to make a living?"

"Good question."

Dwayne hit the last of his balls and joined Tom on a bench at the end of the tees. Tom lit a cigarette.

"Dwayne, here's three bucks. Get us some coffee, will ya?"

"If you're paying, I'm walking."

Tom was going to sift the case right now. It was a good time to think. There was no more Shelly related stress. Last night was the cure. He felt great, clear headed, and he realized how much the situation with Shelly had really been blocking his thought processes.

"You owe me a buck and a half," Dwayne announced.

"What?"

"Coffees are two apiece, tax."

"This guy thinks he's got the snack bar at the movie."

"Same crowd, Tom, captive."

"Coffee two bucks, maybe this business is for us, I mean it."

"Yeah, and this is shitty coffee."

"I like shitty coffee."

"Dwayne, I've got to believe we've seen or been real near this killer."

"How's that?"

"Last night I visited Sugar over there," Tom pointed at the hospital in the distance.

"Sugar told you something?"

"No. But when I left there was a note on my wiper. *Jane was a liar.* That's what it said."

"Got to be our man or a really shitty practical joker."

Practical joker, no way. If any other cop wound me up like that, I'd kill 'im. And they all know that. This was no joke."

"Bad apples?" Dwayne questioned.

"I said bad, not totally rotten. No, this was our man. He must have made me at the scene."

"And me?"

"I've got to think so."

"Shit, you think he followed you?"

"I don't think so. I haven't been my best lately, but I think I would have known. Dan asked me the same thing. I've been thinking about it. I look for a tail as a habit. I didn't realize it, but after Dan's question . . . ."

"So what was he doing at the hospital?" Dwayne asked.

"I didn't even think of that, maybe he was in there. We'll check that out later. Maybe it's a lead, maybe not."

"From the beginning?" Dwayne asked.

"Yeah, from the beginning. Let's talk it slow and easy. I don't want to miss anything."

"Okay, I'll talk, anything I leave out, maybe you'll fill in. Then the other way around, right?" Dwayne said.

"Right, let's nail this thing down."

"Okay Tom, we pulled up to the scene. There were a couple people on the street. A few little kids at the corner store."

"Stop right there. The corner store. Let's remember to check out the regulars and the owner. If any of them just got sober. I'd feel pretty good."

"Why 'just got sober' Tom?"

"Look, don't spread this around. My cousin is in AA. He was totally nuts, when he got there, I mean really crazy. Even dangerous! Well four years later, you'd never know it. That AA stuff really works. He's a new man, a better man than he's ever been. I've got to believe it's someone new, still thinking the old way. Someone who hasn't changed his thinking yet."

"Does everybody get the same results?"

"I can't swear to it, but they must get something out of it."

"Yeah, I guess the crazies don't last."

"Right. That's how it's got to be."

"So you're sure he's in AA."

"I'm feeling good about it. The new angle is a good way to go."

"The corner store is on the same side of the block. You couldn't see the house from inside," Tom said.

"That's right, but we'll still check it out. Dan says this guy saw us there, but from where?"

"All right, I'll continue. There were the crack heads that Clark told off, but that doesn't fit at all," said Dwayne.

"No way! They didn't buy satin sheets. Holy shit, could anyone have been in Mag's mom's before you got there?"

"No, she said she'd talked to no one lately," Dwayne answered.

"Didn't look like she'd had any company?"

"No way, neat as a pin."

"Dwayne, keep talking."

"All right, there was Willis, Clark, Pete Murphy, Dan, Shelly, the ambulance team, but that's about it."

"Did you know the paramedics?" said Tom.

"I didn't even look at them, you were over there," Dwayne said.

"Old timers. They were here when I came to town. Cops no, but let's check out the paramedics. I never trusted people who wanted that job. Creepy bastards," said Tom.

"They're doing an important job, how are they creepy, Tom?"

"They bust their ass to get to car wrecks when they know there are no survivors. Creeps! I know society needs 'em, but they're creeps all the same."

"So check 'em out?" Dwayne asked.

"Absolutely. I guess after you've seen your five-hundredth corpse, you could get a little spooky."

"Long shot!"

"Long shot, agreed. Keep talking."

"We blocked that street. If he was watching, I've got to think he had binoculars."

"Could be, Dwayne. That would make him feel like he was right there. Dan said he'd want that."

"Tom, I guess that's it. I can't think of anything else I saw."

"What about anything you heard? Did anyone say anything odd?" Tom asked.

"No. Everyone just did their job."

"The old lady didn't do it."

Dwayne spilled his coffee and grabbed Tom's arm.

"What have you got?" Tom asked.

"The old lady. When I was in her house, she said 'Look out the window, he's still there.'"

"The Devil, right?" Tom asked.

"No, 'El Diablo' is what she said. Tom, she was a simple-minded old lady. Real lonely, but I didn't get crazy. Just really lonely. Maybe she saw someone she calls 'El Diablo'."

"And he was there, you looked out the window when she told you that, didn't you?"

"I looked out the window, but I didn't look out the window. I just glanced out front."

"Let's go see the lady, and maybe we can take another look out that window."

"Fine Tom, but I'm not going in there."

"Still worried about your ass in a sling?"

"Yeah, Feds suck."

"But we're going in the driving range business, aren't we?" Tom laughed.

"We might have to," Dwayne laughed, too.

Chapter Twenty-seven

Thursday morning 11 AM

They turned off Federal Street to go to the scene of Jane Comfort's murder. Getting into Mrs. Gonzales' house should have been no problem.

"See the van, Tom?"

Dwayne had spotted it instantly. Tom continued to drive by Mrs. Gonzales' house.

"City Root Service, you know they're Feds," Tom said.

"Nobody can get a tradesman with a truck like that down here. It's dirty enough and it has a couple cute dents, but no way is that a repair truck."

"It's got to be a '98."

"The older trucks come down here," Dwayne said.

"What now?" Tom asked.

"What now, indeed. Maybe we should come back later."

"They could be there forever. I'm going to park here, go back around the corner and ask some questions."

"You're going to the house?" Dwayne asked.

"No, to the van. I'm not suicidal, just in a hurry."

"They won't like it, Tom."

"Hey, they don't have to."

"You might mess something up."

"I doubt it. Look Dwayne, while I'm there, check out the grocers. See if he's got a mirror on the outside of the building. Maybe he did watch. Tell him you're trying to quit drinking or something. Try and drop AA into the conversation. You know the deal."

"Do I look like someone with a drinking problem?"

"Yeah, you don't. Say you're brother is the problem or something. Figure it out."

Tom stepped out to go around the corner and up the street. Asphalt beaches, an old partner called the streets asphalt beaches. Everyone outside on a beach chair, radios playing tunes from windowsills, cold beer passed from hand to hand and barbecues with corn and hot dogs. Yup, on a day like this, these streets sometimes resembled asphalt beaches.

Tom saw the van ahead on his side of the street, the right side. He walked steadily toward the van. He stopped to light a cigarette and dropped his lighter. He was certain if anyone was in the van, they would know he was coming. He didn't want to surprise anybody.

Dwayne walked to the store. He watched Tom until he got to the rear of the van. The shop looked open, he walked to the door. It was a small shop, but surprising. Two brothers owned it and kept it up. Well, they kept it up inside. It affected Dwayne much the same way as Maria's house. The floor was replaced within the last five years. Dwayne had done enough work when he was young to tell how correct a job it was. How it was done and what the cost would be. Enough is enough. Someone spent money fixing this place up. Could it be?

"Sir, good morning," the shopkeeper said.

"Morning to you, how about a sausage sandwich?"

"You got it, man."

The grill was right against the rear wall, which was all aluminum and stainless steel. It was a nice setup here. Dwayne wondered how big a crowd they got here. They weren't lining up. This place was way too nice. Dwayne turned and looked out the corner window. He couldn't see the crime scene. Maria's house was the only house you could see from here. Ah, hell yes, it was much too nice.

"You better make it two, they look good," Dwayne said.

"They are good. We've got the best sandwiches in the city."

"You keep your place really nice."

"Thanks, we try. You're one of the new 76er's, aren't you?"

"Well, not yet. I just got into town to talk to Pat and the boys in charge."

"Jamal! Come out here."

"What do you want?" his brother yelled.

"Might have a Sixer out here."

"For real? I'm coming," he called.

"Here's your sandwiches. My name is Saladim."

"Glad to meet you, my name's Dwayne."

"God damn slave name and it fits a man who's working for the man, enslaving the black brothers of the city. He's no Sixer, he's a cop," Jamal stated.

"Really?" Saladim said.

"I don't have time to lie. I'm busy here. Keep the change," said Dwayne as he left the shop. He heard the brothers talking behind him.

"Jamal, you wrong. He's no cop, not in those clothes. Cops don't wear suits like that."

"Maybe I am, maybe I'm not. His clothes say Sixer; his face says cop. I look in the eyes. His eyes were looking for answers."

Dwayne walked around the corner to the car. He glanced over his shoulder, no mirror outside. No, they were watching Mag's stash. It was the only way it fit, nice store, but they'd have to stay really busy to pay for those improvements. They weren't busy. It was almost lunchtime and they had no business.

Tom was walking toward Dwayne from the other corner. He hoped Dwayne had accomplished something, he hadn't. They reached the car at the same time and climbed in.

"How'd you make out, Tom?"

"Well, I got to talk to the Feds."

"What are they doing, babysitting?"

"They wish. Seems like Mag let the boys down. They can't find him."

"You're kidding."

"No Dwayne, they're desperate. I've got a feeling our man Mag screwed them for some money. Big money."

"If they can't find him, he's probably long gone. How much money, I guess they didn't say."

"No, no real information, but I saw a scared look in their faces. They've blown it. I know it."

"Did they ask you why you were there?"

"Yes, they did."

"And?"

"I told them the truth. I just wanted to look out the window and ask the old lady a few more questions."

"You're cruel, Tom. Nothing screws up the Feds more than the truth."

"Right you are. I guarantee you at this moment, in the van, there is a heated conversation."

"Yeah, probably sounds like this . . . . 'What do you think he really wanted? Maybe he's after the stash.'"

"And, 'He's probably working for Mag,'" Tom added.

"Well, if you didn't have a tail before, you probably will now."

"I don't think so. They will go round and round, check us out, then mark us down as dumb city cops. They're worried about the money."

"Would Mag screw with the Feds?" Dwayne asked.

"If he did, he must've done it big. He can't hope to retrieve his stash. The stash is probably a million on the street. He must have hit them big."

"Tom, why does that make me happy?"

"I don't know, but if you figure it out, tell me. I'm happy, too."

"Anything at the corner store?" Tom asked.

"Real nice shop. Real nice. They have a perfect view of Maria's. I've got to believe that they watch the stash," said Dwayne.

"No mirror?"

"No, they can't see that side of the street."

"Were they creepy?" asked Tom.

"No, militant yes, creepy no," said Dwayne.

"Militant?" said Tom.

"Black Muslims, you know. What's a black man doing arresting the black brothers for the man."

"They made you in those clothes?"

"Shocking, isn't it?" smiled Dwayne.

"It is."

"Tom, do I look like a cop?"

"Dwayne, somehow, you do. More, everyday. I can't put my finger on it, but, yes.

"I'm depressed."

"Cheer up, you could look like worse," Tom said.

"I guess, but a cop . . ." Dwayne sighed.

"The Feds are going to hang today if they don't hear from Mag. They're going to take the stash. I guess they figure they can make a deal or something," said Tom.

"Good luck, if Mag hit them big, he's not coming back. He knows he's done in this city. Everybody knows when the Feds are around."

"That's right. In this city, if the dealers even think you're in bed, you're dead. Mag will know he's done."

"He's probably stepping off a plane right now."

"Tropical climate?" Tom asked.

"You bet."

"Puerto Rico?"

"No, they'd expect that."

"Brazil?" asked Tom.

"Could be."

"Those Feds might be kissing our asses for jobs by the end of the week," Tom laughed.

"Federal Government does have a way of destroying it's own agents."

"Famous for it," Tom agreed.

"Great for us if he did split. He handled half the crap coming into the city."

"Beautiful, I like it all the way around," Tom chuckled.

"What about Mrs. Gonzales?"

"I squared them about her, she's an innocent," Tom said.

"No, I meant, when can we go in?" Dwayne asked.

"Tomorrow morning, I want to look out the window, the same time of day. Sunday, the same time, would've been better, but tomorrow is tomorrow."

"We don't see anything tomorrow, come back Sunday."

"That's right," said Tom.

"Got some sausage sandwiches," Dwayne said.

"You got sausage from Muslims?"

"Yeah well, I didn't see them eat it."

"Muslims, yeah, right. A Muslim wouldn't have a sausage in his shop. Oh yeah, they were working for Mag. I wonder if they know they're out of work?"

"I doubt it. Jamal was pretty cocky."

"I bet they're out of business the next month or two," Tom said.

"I wouldn't take that bet."

"Dwayne, do you think the girls are home?" Tom asked.

"No way, but I'll have Shelly call you as soon as they come in."

"Think you're smart, don't you?"

"Yes, I do," Dwayne laughed.

"Okay, have her call me. Let's call it a day. Tomorrow morning at seven, you and I are going to see Maria."

"If we come up blank?" Dwayne asked.

"I feel good about it. I don't think we will."

"I didn't bother with the AA angle at the grocers," Dwayne reported.

"Why not, didn't think you could pull it off?"

"I could have pulled it off. Saladim had booze on his breath. He's not in AA."

"Sausages and booze. Oh hell yeah, they're devout Muslims."

"Willis hates night work, Tom."

"Who doesn't, he'll just have to cope."

"I'll drop you off. I didn't get much sleep last night. It's catching up to me."

"You dog!" Dwayne laughed.

"Think what you will. But you're way off the mark."

"If you say so."

"I do."

Chapter Twenty-eight

Thursday Afternoon 1 PM

Tom decided to swing by Jim's. If he was in, Tom could find out what happened last night, if anything. More importantly, he had to decide to tell Jim that it was likely the killer was a guy in AA. A new guy. Pretty risky, no, he'd get some information somehow. No, for now anyway.

The truck was there. He pulled up to the curb. Lex, the Rottweiler, was on the porch on a six-foot chain. A chair was on the porch, with today's paper on it. A cup of coffee still steamed. Tom thought Jim must have seen him coming.

"Yo, Jim!" Tom shouted past the now barking dog.

"Relax. I saw you coming. I got something on the stove. You want coffee?" he shouted out the door.

"Okay."

The dog had stopped barking. It just stared at Tom. Clearly, it would not be smart to walk up on the porch. Tom knew that until Jim commanded, *lay down,* that dog was on duty. He'd wait.

"Lay down," Jim shouted.

The dog walked next to his chair and lay down. Still staring at Tom.

"Here's your coffee."

"You just getting up?"

"Woke up at noon, just getting going, though. Late night at the casino."

"Went down last night, huh?"

"Oh yeah, and it was about time. I kicked the shit out of 'em."

"Win big?"

"Forty-nine hundred . . . roulette. I'm done working for two weeks. I'm going to Canada fishing. Been on the phone for a half hour setting it up."

"Hey, that's great. What were you playing, numbers or colors?"

"I was playing numbers and man, I was hot. Eight spins in a row, I hit with twenty on a number."

"That's fifty-six hundred."

"I know, but you're spending a hundred a spin, oh, they get it back even while you're winning. But it was a great night. But I don't guess you came here about that."

"That's great. You deserve a vacation. When you leaving?" Tom asked.

"Monday at eight ten a.m., rain or shine."

"Flying?"

"No, I like the trains, if you have the time, they're still the greatest way to go."

"They still have poker."

"I'm counting on it."

"Trophy fish, maybe?" Tom hemmed.

"Okay, Tom, you were polite, I forgive you. I'm in too good a mood to stay angry. Ask your questions."

"I've got a couple," Tom smiled.

"A couple shit; with you that means ten."

"No way ten."

"At least six."

"Probably," Tom laughed.

"I went to the meeting last night. A lot of talk about Jane; nothing about Marco. I'm not going to learn anything there. I'm done going. Gives me the creeps."

"Jim, they found Marco in the river. His head was smashed in . . . murder."

"No shit!"

"No shit, he didn't kill Jane, but he bought the bike that was found at the crime scene."

"What bike?"

"It doesn't matter, but the killer left a bike by Jane's body."

"Sounds weird. You never told me much about where you found her. Was she bad?"

"You liked her. I'd tell you if I thought it would help the case."

"Was it horrible?" Jim asked.

"Yes, it was."

"It wouldn't help me to know?"

"I don't think so."

"Spare me, then."

"You're spared."

Tom was instantly sorry he gave that promise. He might have to tell him. It might lead somewhere. If he had met the person capable of this crime, he should be memorable.

"So this Marco was tied into Jane's murder. Maybe there were two guys and one killed the other to shut him up."

"I don't think so. I think the killer probably knew this Marco. At least, good enough to pay him to go buy a bike. This kid Marco was doing bad. I don't think he would have turned down twenty bucks to go buy a bike."

"The killer sends him to buy the bike, then murders him."

"Looks like it," said Tom.

"You think the killer is in AA."

"It looks likely," said Tom.

"I can't believe it. There are a lot of numbskulls in there, but this . . . how could that be. He kills two people and then walks in there and says the Lord's Prayer with Jane's friends. Who could be that weird?"

"That's my question for you. Jim, I know that AA has helped millions of people pull their lives together. Many have become very successful. My family has a member, and we know what it has done for him. But any group of people that large . . . come on, it's possible."

"Anything's possible," Jim said.

"Heck yeah, hell, they just arrested a District Attorney in Delaware for murder. You're right. Nowadays, anything is possible. So think, Jim, take your time. Do you know anyone that weird? Probably someone who hasn't been there that long."

"Hasn't been there that long, I can't tell you much about the people that haven't been around long."

"Did you see anyone strange?"

"How strange?"

"Like the devil."

"Half the time people say I look like the devil. How's this guy strange? What am I looking for?" said Jim.

"Okay, okay. Someone really weird. Maybe cold or a quiet loner."

"That could fit a lot of people."

"I know it, but this guy is there. I feel it. What did Jane and Marco have in common?"

"Not much. She was beautiful; he wasn't. She had friends; he didn't. She was popular; he wasn't. They both went to AA meetings."

"Exactly. They did have that in common. Anything else . . . dance partners . . . anything?"

"They *are* members of the same *home group*."

"What's *home group*?"

"Want some more coffee?"

"Got any beer?"

"No! I'll get you coffee." Jim walked inside.

Tom liked it. Jane and Marco were members of the same home group. He didn't know how many members that group had. One of the members could be the killer. Every case had a link. Finding it was the trick. Maybe this was the link. Every group member was now a suspect. Tom thought maybe fifty members. He'd gone to a meeting once to hear his cousin speak at the front of a room. He'd been sober one year. There had been about fifty people at that meeting. It shouldn't be too hard, with that small a number. He was pumped.

"Here's your coffee. You hungry?"

"I ate. Thanks for the coffee. Look Jim, anyway you could find out how many people are in that home group?"

"I know."

"What?" Tom asked.

"There's about eight. I went to the diner with them after the meeting, the first meeting you sent me to."

"Only eight?"

"Maybe ten, they don't all show up."

"Ten." Tom smiled.

"You think the killer's one of the home group."

"You've only got ten people in your mind, that group at the diner. Sit back and tell me who's the weirdo in the group. Just sit back and think. Just sit back close your eyes and think," said Tom.

Jim leaned back. Tom wondered if Dan's method would work for Jim as promptly as it had worked on himself.

"I'm not sure if he's in the home group, no, you said someone new."

"Yes, probably new."

"Nobody struck me as weird in the group."

"Jim, everyone gets back in shape fast there, right? I mean the people that have been sober a long time are trustworthy, right?"

"On the whole, absolutely."

"There are exceptions?" Tom asked.

"Hell, yes."

"I'd really like to get a look at that group," said Tom.

"With or without them knowing it?"

"I think, without."

"Most of them will probably be at the Thursday night meeting at the church in Westville. There's a set of stairs down to the basement. Only way in and out. Find a good spot."

"Perfect, you've got to go with me."

"Tom, I wouldn't feel right about it."

"You worried you'll be seen with me?"

"Yeah, I am. Not for any bad reasons. But these people, some of them, more than I really want to admit, are people I've learned to love. I couldn't do it."

"I can fix it. We can watch the show from a couple blocks away," said Tom.

"A couple of blocks, beautiful."

"What time does the meeting start?"

"Between three and three-thirty will be the best time to hide a camera."

"Great, I was getting at that. Still, I've got to know what time you and I are going to be there."

"We should catch everyone between eight and nine o'clock."

"It's for Jane's killer. If they knew, they'd understand."

"Some would never understand," said Jim.

"What time should I pick you up?"

"Seven-thirty."

"See you then." Tom got up to leave.

The dog was up. "Lay down Lex. Tom, you're no fun anymore."

"I know it," said Tom.

Chapter Twenty-nine

Thursday Evening 5 PM

Tom was tired and hot. It hadn't been so easy to hide the camera. He couldn't find a moment alone. Someone was always around. Finally, he got an idea. He bought a nice boxwood and hid the camera in the shrub. Then, he'd gone to Dan's house, got the Lincoln and Dan, and went back to the church. They got out of the car. The Parsonage was on the far side of the church. If Tom was quick, it should work.

Tom dug a small hole and Dan dropped the plant in the hole. Tom checked the angle of the camera. It would be perfect. A bird's eye view of anyone going down those stairs would be his. Tom drove around the church while Dan stood at the top of the stairs. He checked the picture on the screen in the Lincoln. Perfect! Wally Yost had set the whole gimmick up for Tom. He was a P.I. and he could bug or peep any location. Tom owed him one. The picture was good, but it would be better after dark. Tom was adjusting the picture.

Dan was talking to an old lady with a dog. Maybe she was looking for a man. Dan seemed a little uncomfortable. Tom would go around and bail him out. The camera was working fine.

"Smooth, wasn't it, Dan?"

"It worked well. We looked like a couple of Christians, doing our bit to beautify the church."

"What did the old lady want?"

"Believe it or not, sex."

"What?" Tom chuckled.

"She wanted me to come across the street for a little while, and have a drink. She said her daughter wouldn't be home for an hour."

"Want me to swing back around and wait for you?"

"No thank you, I've done my good deed for the day," said Dan.

"See, you've still got it, Dan."

"Somehow, being attractive to women your own age, at my age, doesn't ring your bell," Dan said.

"I don't know, she looked pretty hot?"

"Can it clown, she was on some pretty heavy Meds. She needs a keeper."

"If she was fifty?" Tom chuckled.

"Then, I'd have you swing back around."

"Worked like a charm, didn't it?"

"I thought the kid that walked by was going to help you dig the hole," Dan said.

"We looked like we were supposed to be there."

"You'll have to get the camera tonight. You know the new bush will be noticed soon. The clergy have a pretty small world. They know every blade of grass at that church."

"As long as it's not noticed for five hours, I'll be happy," Tom smiled.

"If they see it, they'll probably think it was done by someone trying to help the church; they won't move it right away. It could be from a large contributor."

"You jaded old bastard; you're probably right."

"Car runs great, doesn't it?"

"Sure does, Dan. Thanks again."

"I'm glad you like it."

"I've got to get over to Dwayne's, to pick up Shelly, you want to go? Or should I drop you off?" Tom asked.

"I'll take the ride. There's a good view from his balcony and this will be my last chance to see South Jersey."

"When you leaving, Dan?" asked Tom.

"I was going to wait until next week, but my brother's so excited, I'm leaving tomorrow. He's two years older than I am. If I don't get there soon, he might have a stroke."

"Don't say that, Dan."

"He's always been excitable, it's possible. I'm going tomorrow."

"I thought we'd get together at least one evening for drinks."

"You're getting married to Shelly, correct?" said Dan.

"Correct."

"We'll have more evenings together," said Dan.

"Tel Aviv?" Tom asked.

"Tel Aviv."

"Am I going to have any say in what we do?"

"Not much, but she's a lot smarter than you. When you marry a good Jewish woman, just go along, it will work out better."

"The wisdom of your years, Dan?"

"No, just common sense."

They both laughed. Shelly would have her way and they both knew it would be the right way.

"Dan, I've been thinking of retiring," Tom said.

"Because of Shelly?"

"No, because I'm sick of it."

"Then you're doing the right thing. What are your plans?"

"Well, Dwayne thinks we should open a driving range. You know anything about that business?"

"Yes. Location, location, location."

"That's it?"

"That's it, in the right spot you make a fortune," said Dan.

"The right spot is probably really expensive."

"Probably, but you could swing it."

"Maybe, maybe not. What do you think we'd need to open?"

"To be comfortable, two million."

"Two million! That's the end of that idea."

"You're surprised?"

"Hell yes. I thought half a million tops."

"In a good location, ten acres of land is going to cost half a million."

"Well, I'll think of something else," said Tom.

"Don't be so fast to throw in the towel."

"It's in the ring. I can't raise that kind of money."

"Dwayne probably doesn't have it either, so don't feel bad."

"It was a crazy idea. Cop talk, that's all," said Tom.

"Yeah, cop talk," Dan smiled.

Tom pulled up to Dwayne's condo. Everyone was out on the balcony. They looked like they had a good day.

"I'll miss this crazy state," Dan said.

"I guess you can get fond of anyplace."

"New Jersey's really nice, Tom. Aside from the San Francisco area, there's no place in the States I'd rather live."

"You're kidding. What about North Carolina? You have a place down there."

"Just for fishing. Snakes, bugs and hurricanes. You can keep it. No, New Jersey is about as good as it gets," said Dan.

"I saw a valley in Idaho, once," Tom said.

"Oh, it's beautiful out West, but I need a crowd."

"Tel Aviv should be heaven for you."

"Absolutely," smiled Dan.

They climbed out of the car. Tom knew it would probably be their last talk for a while. Dan must have read his mind.

"Tom, why the long face? Telephone."

"How about that, telephone!"

They walked up to the building. They were good friends and they would stay good friends. It didn't need to be said.

The doorman was off duty. Tom rang Dwayne's buzzer. They were buzzed in.

"Hi Tom, Dan, come in." Dwayne greeted.

"Hello everyone," Dan called.

Doris' father was busy on the balcony. His cooking was famous. It mirrored his appetite. Shelly walked in with Doris. Shelly took Tom's arm and Doris gave Dwayne a casual hug.

"Hi Shelly, have fun? Hi Doris," Tom said.

"I guess we had fun, what do you say, Doris?"

"If I can shop with someone else's money, it's fun," Doris said.

"Dwayne, I guess I didn't get you home in time to stop the trip to the stores."

"What makes you think we wouldn't have gone if Dwayne were here?" Shelly asked.

"That's right, Tom. A woman has to shop sometime," Doris smiled.

"Well Dwayne, I talked to Dan about the driving range. Can't be done, as things are, at least on my end."

"As it happens, I asked the same thing of Daddy. He said it would take about two or three, Dwayne said.

"Dan said the same. Oh, Well."

"So what's up, Tom?" Dwayne asked.

"Yeah, what's up?" Shelly also asked.

"I really have to be somewhere in about an hour. Something to do with the case. I feel like this case has a place to focus."

"So why do I feel like Dwayne's going to have to eat his dinner fast," Doris said.

"I'm sorry Doris, but I want his input. I'm taking someone outside the force with me, it's just smart have two cops with him. For a lot of reasons, I'm sure you'll ask Dwayne to explain to you later."

"Thanks, Tom, she'll remember that," Dwayne said.

"Don't feel alone Dwayne, when Tom has the time, he can explain them to me," Shelly smiled.

"Well boys, have fun. Shelly and I just chilled some wine and I for one, intend to enjoy," Doris said.

"This doesn't change our plans, Doris," Shelly stated.

"What time will you be home, Dwayne?" Doris asked.

"Tom?" Dwayne said.

"Nine thirty, we could be back by nine thirty."

"Oh, Shelly you're in trouble. He's such a liar," Doris laughed.

"All right, ten o'clock," Tom laughed.

"I was going to introduce Dan to your father, Doris, but it seems like they're old friends."

"Dan makes friends fast when they can cook," Shelly laughed.

"It does smell good. Got enough?"

"For the building!" Dwayne laughed.

"Dwayne, stop it," Doris said.

"It is a lot of food, honey."

"Just as long as you don't say anything about Daddy."

"Never crossed my mind."

They all walked to the balcony to wait for the cook at the grill to give the all clear. Tom could see Dwayne wanted to talk. Tom greeted Doris' father, drooled at the food, then saw Dan was enjoying the view.

"Shelly, Doris, please excuse us for about one minute?" Tom asked.

"Case; go on," Shelly said.

"Go on in, but Dwayne, don't go without your dinner," Doris said.

"We're just going in the other room," Dwayne said.

"Don't trust him, Doris?" Shelly asked.

"Oh, I trust him, but he's a man," Doris laughed and so did Shelly.

"Great isn't it?" Shelly laughed.

"Yes it is," Doris agreed.

Tom followed Dwayne into the kitchen. He could see out the sliding glass door. The wine and the food were calling, this would be quick.

"Tom, what's up?" Dwayne asked.

"Jane and Marco were in the same home group. "

"What's that?"

"I don't know, really. But it's the only thing they have in common. Jim is going with us to finger the group. I want you along for your opinion. One of this group could be the killer."

"It's a tie, and sometimes, a tie can win," Dwayne smiled.

"You've been hanging with Jim. That's what he sounds like when he talks."

"Bets sports?" Dwayne asked.

"Sports and other things," said Tom.

"Let's be polite and join the crowd," Dwayne said.

"And eat!" Tom smiled.

Chapter Thirty

Thursday night 8 PM Meeting

Jim climbed into the Town Car.

"Hi Jim, this is Dwayne."

"Hey Dwayne, Tom," said Jim.

"I hope that barbecue I smell isn't just on your tie, Tom," Jim said.

"We come prepared. Had to cut dinner short," Dwayne said.

"We didn't cut dinner short, we were laughing too hard to eat," Tom said.

"Everything working all right, Tom? Jim asked.

"It was when I checked it."

"What did you check, Tom?" Dwayne asked.

"The camera."

"You got permission to spy at a church?"

"No. Officially, there's no camera here."

"I wish I wasn't here," Dwayne said.

"Relax. No way can we get caught," said Tom.

"What if someone finds the camera?" Jim asked.

"We drive away, leave it. Can't be traced," Tom said.

"Isn't that what the bad guys are supposed to say?" Dwayne asks.

"Everything will be all right. I do this stuff all the time."

"Dwayne's not used to your methods. Good for you Dwayne! Don't let this guy get you in trouble," Jim chuckled.

"I don't intend to. I don't know about any camera and I'll swear to that."

"He causes me to swear all the time, don't let him get you started," Jim said.

"Thanks a lot, Jim. Dwayne, feed him something," said Tom.

"Won't work, Tom, I do some of my best talking with my mouth full."

"All right, we're almost there. It's seven forty-five, we're on time, right?"

"Right, they'll be dribbling in any minute," replied Jim.

"Dwayne, Jim's going to point out the group members. Take a good look at these people, our guy might be here."

"I still don't think so, Tom," Jim said.

"Then no harm's done and you ate for free."

"Tom, you're so thoughtful," Jim mocked.

"All right, let me check the equipment."

"Jim, Tom get you in many jams?" Dwayne asked.

"Out of some."

"That's the best thing I heard; I like the Force," Dwayne said.

"It's working. Jim, scoot up and keep your eyes open," Tom said.

"Your car Tom?" Jim asked.

"Yes it is."

"How do you cops do it?" Jim asked.

"It's stolen, don't worry, I'm not on the take." Tom smiled at Dwayne.

"Oh, that's good," Jim said.

"How about that guy, Jim?" Tom asked.

"He's coming out for a smoke, probably comes early to make coffee. I don't know him. Look, I'll point them out; there might be a hundred people here tonight. Let's not go through this on every one, okay?" Jim asked.

"A hundred people? What's down there, Bingo?" Dwayne asked.

"Bingo's last night," Jim said.

"Big meeting, a hundred," Tom said.

"About ten good looking girls come here regular. That draws the ninety men," Jim said.

"She's got to be one of them, she looks like a kid," Dwayne said.

"That pretty bitch has no fucking heart. She'll do great in AA. Most guys just can't get past her sex appeal," Jim said.

"You know her, Jim?" Tom asked.

"Lived with her for three months, I'm cured."

"That bad?" Dwayne asked.

"She fucks people she meets at a red light."

"She new, Jim?" Tom asked.

"No. But I don't think she belongs here. Her problem ain't alcohol, it's sex."

"But how long has she been coming to these things?" Tom asked.

"About five years."

"Five years, good night nurse."

"Tom, our man might not be new," Dwayne said.

"I guess not, but it doesn't matter. We'll take a look at all the members of that group."

"How about that creep?" Tom asked.

"I told you I'd point them out," Jim said.

"But that guy was really strange. What do you know about him?"

"Only a little."

"Well, what is it?" asked Tom.

"Relax Tom, you might not want to hear it," Jim smiled.

"Let's hear it, already."

"He preaches here on Sunday," Jim laughed.

"He's the Reverend?" Dwayne asked.

"Yeah, he's probably going down to collect the night's rent. I think we can take him off the list. Hey, that's Juno, he's in the group, and Margie, she's another."

"Umm," Tom groaned.

"Look at this woman, she's beautiful," Dwayne said.

"And deadly," Jim added.

"Deadly, how so?" Tom asked.

"H.I.V."

"Damn shame," Tom said.

"There's Pauly and Shane. They're in the group."

"Are they gay?" Tom asked.

"No, bisexual," Jim said.

"That's close enough," Dwayne said.

"That's Rene and Rachael, they love everybody. They're nice. They've been around a long time," Jim said.

"I'll give them the benefit of the doubt," Tom said.

"Big of ya, one's got a walker. The other's got a cane," Jim said.

They watched for a few minutes. Tom was surprised by the ages; from fourteen to one hundred. All races. Time slowly moved to eight fifteen.

"From Yale to jail. Drunks don't come from one slice of life," Jim said.

"Yale to jail," Dwayne repeated.

"That's Bruce and Gail. How many is that, Tom? I don't think many more people will be coming. This crowd likes to be on time."

"That's eight," Tom said.

"I said eight to ten, yeah, that's it," said Jim.

"Shit, what are you doing later, Jim?" asked Tom.

"I got a girl coming over, she ain't too good looking, but she's willing."

"Never mind. I'll come back tomorrow morning for the camera," Tom said.

"There is one more guy that might be in the group. He works nights. After the girl splits, I could ask him his home group."

"What's his name and how long has he been sober?" Tom asked.

"His name is Ron P . . . ten years."

"How do the people here find a friend if he's in the hospital. *I'm looking for Mike F.?* It doesn't work, does it?" asked Tom.

"That's always a problem," Jim said.

"It's stupid. What are they ashamed of?" Tom said.

"They're ashamed of their drinking. That's why it's *Anonymous*," Jim said.

"Yeah, right, right. This guy that's sober ten years, what's he do?" Tom asked.

"He drives a cab," Jim said.

"Cab drivers make a lot of money around here?" Dwayne asked.

"Not much, but they get by."

"You can go see him, but I doubt he's our man," Tom said.

"I don't like him," Jim said.

"Why not?"

"I don't know, I don't like most of the people I meet."

"Well there's red hot news. You punch most of the people you meet," said Tom.

"Bullshit," Jim said.

"I still think AA's good for this guy. He doesn't have to be in that group," said Tom.

"Home group!" Jim said.

"Okay, home group," Tom said.

"I tried Tom, but that's it for me. I've got a ticket to ride, I'm packing for Canada," Jim said.

"Thanks Jim, I guess we tried."

"Look Tom, I hope you get the guy. But I don't have a clue."

"We did try and that's what matters," Dwayne said.

"Relax Dwayne, we're out of here. Wait till I see Doris, we'll be back by nine thirty," Tom laughed.

"Who cooked this food? He's not from around here," Jim asked.

"My father-in-law. He's from Florida."

"He looking for a roommate? I'd live with anyone who cooks like this," said Jim.

"I'll ask him," Dwayne said.

"Jim, be careful tonight," Tom said.

"This guy wouldn't hurt a fly. He'd cheer if you killed one, but I don't think he could do it."

"Real pussy?" Tom asked.

"He never drank in any bar I liked."

"Well, Dwayne, we've still got Maria's house. Another shot likely to come up empty," said Tom.

"Seven A.M.?" Dwayne asked.

"Seven A.M.," Tom said.

"You taking the dog with you Jim?" Tom asked.

"No way. He's a homebody. He's got a job to do. The little girl up the street has a key. She'll look after Mr. Lex."

"That kid's only about eleven."

"Ten, but they're old friends, Lex would never hurt a kid, he's smart."

"Why does he always want to kill me?" Tom asked.

"You oil your gun?"

"Yes."

"He's trained to guard against anyone who smells of it. Anybody without a gun, I ain't worried about."

"No shit," Tom said.

"None at all."

Tom was thinking about Shelly and about sleep. He was beat. It had been a long day. Dwayne was wondering if Big Daddy was still eating. He'd know in twenty minutes. Jim's house wasn't out of the way.

Jim was sure Ron would be by the Speed Line tonight. Jim would stop by about twelve, after his lady left. It was odd that he didn't know the last name of someone he hadn't liked for the last ten years. He'd ask Ron his last name tonight.

Chapter Thirty-one

Thursday night, Midnight

Jim was on the front porch with Lex. He'd just said goodbye to a nice girl. He wondered why he didn't marry her. She was nice, friendly. Shit, the dog even liked her. He would keep this setup as long as she'd put up with it. Anyway, they're all nice, until you live with them.

Maybe he'd just take a little trip down AC later. His luck might still be running. Now he'd go look for the creep. That's it, though. He figured he was even with Tom. No more meetings.

He drove the truck slowly through town. He liked the late hours. No traffic, not much noise. He liked a lot of things lately, but so much for the good mood. He imagined what Jane looked like when they found her; the hell with this. He turned on the radio. The air was cool. He should have brought Lex. No, he'd been having gas problems. Better Jim left Lex at home. Nothing smells worse than a Rotty with gas.

A girl in Spandex was getting in her car in front of the diner. She waved to him; he pulled into the lot.

"Hi Jimmy."

"Hi."

"What have you been doing?"

"Not much, same old stuff."

"Still roofing?"

"What else, it's all I know."

"Going with anyone?"

"Nobody will have me."

"Look, I've got a girl friend with me. Why don't you stop by tomorrow night, it's Friday."

"What time?"

"About eight."

"Great!" Jim smiled.

"See you tomorrow."

He watched her drive away. This was great. He wouldn't be a shithead this time. What luck. He was definitely going to the casino. First, the creep. Maybe Jim would give him a scare. Jim was in a good mood and this guy wasn't the one.

What luck, meeting her. He felt great.

Maybe he wouldn't go to the casino. He realized why he had been gambling so much. He had four twenty-five dollar chips in his ashtray. He turned and drove back to the diner. A lady named Jane had worked there thirty years. He knew she was about to retire.

He walked into the diner.

"Jim, you sober?" Jane yelled from behind the counter.

He laughed. She was a real nice lady.

"Has it been that long since I've been in here?" Jim smiled.

"Last time you were here, it took two cops to drag you out."

"For Pete's sake Janey, that was nine or ten years ago."

"If you say so, but it seems like yesterday to me."

"Was I that bad?" he asked.

"In a word, yes."

"Here Jane, for your retirement, my lucky chips."

"Four quarters, thanks Jim. I always said you were my favorite drunk."

"See you later Janey."

"Don't be a stranger."

He walked out, there was no point telling her he didn't drink. She wouldn't believe it anyway. He was used to her way of looking at him. A lot of people still looked at him that way. He didn't care. The lucky chips were gone and he knew he wouldn't be spending his nights in Atlantic City, anymore. He had another chance; he'd use it well.

Jim cruised around. He went past the Speed Line. Two cabs were there, not the cab he wanted to see. He'd try Collingswood Speed Line, about three miles up the line. Ron could be there.

As Jim drove out Haddon Avenue, he saw someone limping along about two blocks ahead. He knew it was Bad Leg John. Old drinking buddies don't die, or this son of a bitch would be dead. Jesus, he was still wearing the same clothes, or perfect replicas, probably the same. This loser was a mess. Against Jim's better judgement, he'd give the guy a ride. Jim *did* feel benevolent.

"That you, John?"

"Who's that?" John yelled, as he put his hand in his jacket pocket.

"You won't need that knife, John," said Jim.

"That you, Jim? Thank God."

Jim pulled over and John limped to the truck. He thought his leg must be getting worse. He walked stiffly. Jim thought he might regret this move. John slowly climbed into the truck. Jim pulled away from the curb.

"Jim, I had an accident," John said.

"Who would let *you* drive their car?" Jim laughed.

"Not that kind of accident," John said.

"For Pete's sake John, get out and get in back."

"If you could just take me to the motel," John said.

"In back now or I punch your face!"

"All right. I'll get out, but don't leave me," John begged.

"I won't leave you, asshole!"

John climbed out and got in the back of the truck. Jim was laughing. He remembered the same accident. He'd had that wreck too many times to forget. Beer all day, nothing to eat; John had shit his pants. Jim remembered how much fun he'd had drinking . . . not much. He drove about a half-mile to a motel. Laughing the entire way at John. He thought John was going to cry and didn't blame him. Once upon a time, Jim would have made the most of this situation. He would have humiliated John. John didn't know that Jim had changed. Probably thought he was going to drop him off, full of shit and in the middle of nowhere. Once, Jim would have done just that. He pulled into the motel.

"Get out, John."

"I don't know if I can cover the room."

"Here's fifty, get sober ya slob."

"Thanks Jim, you're okay."

"Fuck you, get sober."

Jim drove back down the road toward the Speed Line. John looked like he was getting what he paid for . . . misery.

Jim thought John had to be the sorriest old biker he knew. But there were probably sorrier, Jim just didn't know them.

1 AM Friday Morning

He pulled into Collingswood Speed Line. Ron's cab was there. One o'clock Friday morning. Jim thought, nineteen hours until I'm with her again, after all these years. God was great, and smart. He hadn't given her back until Jim was ready. 'God's will, not mine be done.' Jim finally understood.

He would have some fun with Ron, shake him up a little and go home. Then Jim thought he'd get her something nice tomorrow. She wouldn't care about that. That's why he'd do it, because *he* cared. He pulled up behind Ron and blew his horn. It sounded loud against the empty train station.

"Yo Ron, what have you been up to?"

"What do you mean? What are you doing here?"

"Look Ron, this big cop I know thinks you might have killed Jane." Jim tried to keep a straight face, but he could see the coward shaking.

"I can prove I didn't. Look at this."

Jim leaned into the window of the cab. The train was screaming past the station.

"God's will," Ron said.

Jim fell back on the pavement. He knew he'd been shot. He knew he was dying.

"But I've got a date tonight," he croaked.

Ron didn't get out of the cab. He drove away slowly, looking around for someone, anyone. No witnesses. He didn't like this. How'd the cop figure it? He would ask God later. But right now, Ron saw him, Sammy, out doing his late night rounds at the dumpster behind the market. Sammy wasn't going to cash in those cans. Ron stepped on the gas hard. Sammy was trapped behind the strip mall and a long cyclone fence. Ron aimed the car for the old man. Sammy tried to dodge one way, but as the car approached, he just stood there with his hands together and his eyes closed. Ron hit him doing sixty. Sammy was gone. Ron turned around and checked the body. Sammy was done, good. Ron had been lucky here, but this cop had it figured.

How could he know? Ron smashed his hands on the wheel. How? Maybe the cop just suspected; he couldn't know. Ron would get rid of that gun. After all, he could afford it; he had plenty. He'd wash the car, take a shower and burn his clothes.

Ron had forgotten he was doing God's will. This must just be a test to see if he had the nerve for all the jobs yet to be done. That had to be it. Ron would ask Him later. But first, Ron would burn the car and report it stolen.

Shit! The camera. The way it was hidden it would take a little time to get it out. Shit, all these problems. He wondered what else he'd forgotten.

He thought of Jim's face. He'd known Ron killed Jane, just for a second, but he'd known. That was really good. Eye contact was dead on. He realized he should be grateful for that. God didn't give Ron many gifts. He'd have to remember to appreciate them all. No way the cop knew, was there? He wondered.

Why hadn't Mag called him? Mag would know what to do. He always called on Thursdays to set up the weekend drug run from his mother's house. That scum must have told this cop about Jane; he thought he could trust Mag. He'd killed some people himself. He probably gave Ron up to cover his own ass. He was my only real friend, now this. That had to be it. It made perfect sense. Ron knew it.

Ron thought of his father. God spoke to him. "Like father, like son." He knew what he had to do and how it would end. Somehow Ron realized, he'd always known how it would end.

Chapter Thirty-two

Friday Morning 6:30 AM

"We're coming out, everyone decent?" Doris called.

"Give us a second, Honey," Shelly said.

"Good morning, Tom, Shelly kissed him."

"Good morning, Darling. I don't remember going to bed. We're at Dwayne's," Tom groaned.

"I can see you'll be real sharp today."

"Dan's going away party; we had it here," Tom said.

"Good boy, you're coming around," she laughed.

They got up and dressed. Shelly called the all clear to Doris. She came out wearing a beautiful silk kimono.

"What a party. That Dan has some great stories, grizzly, but funny," Doris said.

"Tom, Shelly, morning," Dwayne said, as he staggered down the hallway.

"How long did I sleep, Honey?" Dwayne asked.

"Four hours and that's all you're getting today. There are a million things to do with the wedding. Shelly! One week! How can we do it?" Doris asked.

"It's going to be a simple wedding, not like yours. We'll be fine. We'll go to Philly, get a nice dress and some shoes. I'm not going crazy."

"We'll see," Doris smiled.

"Tom, I think Shelly will need a truck if she goes shopping with Doris," Dwayne said.

"Stop it, Dwayne. Go back and look in on Daddy and Dan," Doris said.

Dwayne walked back down the hall.

"Doris, excuse me, I need the bath."

"You're excused. Shelly, I was looking at some catalogs last night. I've got some great ideas for a simple wedding."

"As long as the Philadelphia Orchestra isn't involved," Shelly laughed.

"Everyone has the wrong opinion of me. I shop a lot, but I take a lot back," Doris pouted.

"They're having a snoring contest, Daddy's winning by a nose." Dwayne said.

"Let them sleep, Dwayne. They did most of the entertaining," Doris said.

"They did, didn't they," Shelly chuckled.

"How do you feel, Tom?" Dwayne asked as he entered the room.

"I can't answer that in mixed company," Tom said.

"You boys sit down and have coffee, you've got to get going," Doris said.

"They just want to get rid of us, Tom," said Dwayne.

"I looked in the mirror. I don't blame them," he answered.

"Stop it Dwayne, you know that's not true, sometimes."

"I'm sorry, Honey, give me a kiss."

"Stop it Dwayne, sit down and have your coffee. Tom you had somewhere to be this morning, remember?" said Doris.

"That's right. Drink up, Dwayne. I want to be there at seven. Shelly, I'll miss you today."

"Good, I like that," she said.

"You see, Dwayne, how sweet he is to her?" Doris said.

"They ain't married yet," Dwayne chuckled.

"Dwayne!" Doris said.

"Just kidding, Honey."

"You kid too much. Don't listen to him, Tom, and don't change."

Tom pulled Shelly into his lap.

"I won't, Doris."

"I think I'm going to cry," Doris said.

"You are very sentimental, aren't you Sweety?" Shelly said.

"Sentimental is good," Doris sniffled.

"You ready, Tom? I see I'm getting in trouble here," Dwayne said.

"I'm sorry, Honey, weddings effect me this way," Doris ran to the bedroom in tears.

"I'll be right back. I better go cheer her up," Dwayne said.

"How's the case going, Tom? We couldn't talk about it last night," Shelly asked.

"It's not going well. I don't have a suspect. But I think he went to those meetings, maybe not."

"It's only been six days. Keep your chin up," Shelly said.

"It looked good for a while, but last night, those people looked so normal."

"Jeffrey Dahmer looked normal."

"What's that got to do with this?"

"I thought you knew. He went to AA meetings."

"Wow, really?"

"Really."

"He did look normal, didn't he?"

"Yup."

"I've got a lot more work to do than I thought. I figured someone who did something like that . . ."

"Horns and a tail, huh?"

"Yeah. I guess. At least crossed eyes or something," Tom laughed.

"Honey, you can't get them all."

"I don't want them all, just this one. Shelly, I'm going to retire, take my pension."

"The job?"

"The job. Dan made up my mind for me. All the old guard is giving it up. I don't fit in anymore."

"Grandmom would be proud of you."

"Of me? Why?"

She said, "Never keep a job you don't like."

"I like her. Someday tell me everything she said."

"I will, bank on it." Shelly kissed Tom.

"Tom, you ready?" Dwayne asked.

"Yeah, how's Doris?" Tom replied.

"Still crying, but she loves it."

"Dwayne, now I'm telling you to stop it," Shelly laughed.

"See you later Shelly, be careful in the city," said Tom.

"You be careful. Here, take more coffee, both of you," Shelly said.

They walked out to the elevator. The coffee had its work cut out for it. The wine was great and they'd had plenty.

"Tom, your stomach hurt?"

"Yes, I guess it was the laughing."

"A good party."

"A real good party; all my favorite people."

"You don't have many, do you?"

"I can think of a few more," said Tom.

"Look, we're starting nights tonight. We're checking Maria's house, then I'll bring you back. I need sleep," Tom said.

"No argument."

"I doubt we'll get El Diablo."

"So do I," They laughed.

"I think I'll ask Jim to be my best man. After all, I still need a new roof." Tom said.

"You rat."

"I'm just joking, hell, we were friends since grade school. He's had a tough life. He'll like it."

"Dwayne, you mind driving?"

"No, but I'm not promising anything."

"Hell, you'll do better than I could."

"I doubt it, but I'll drive."

"I wonder if she's up," Tom said.

"Old people get up early, she's probably washing her dishes from breakfast."

"I hope she's cooking breakfast," Tom said.

"Me, too."

.   .   .

Ron was at home now. He was at peace for the first time in his life. Now life had meaning, now it made sense. He'd spoken to God. His answer was simple and true. "Like father, like son". He knew he wouldn't speak to God again. His will was plain. All through the years, he'd tried to forget; even to deny it had happened, but it had. Like father, like son. It rang in his head like a bell, but it was a comforting sound. Almost like his mother's voice calling him home. Ron was five when his father had come home drunk, beat his mother and himself. Then his father had walked down the street shooting everyone he had seen. Old men, women, kids, everyone. Like father, like son. Ron's head rang. Walk of Death, the newspapers dubbed it. He remembered his mother's suicide a month later. He remembered being in foster homes one after the other. He'd remembered the shame. He never had a real friend. Just Mag, and now he had betrayed him.

Ron was sure God had carried him all these years for this day. God was angry, and he would be His tool. No one was innocent. No one was forgiven. Ron wondered how it would unfold. He was grateful for one thing. When he'd won the Cash Five Lottery, Mag had set him up with full body armor, grenades, two good rifles and two pistols. It had cost almost the whole prize. But now, he saw it was God's will. Ron wouldn't be as easy to stop as his father had been, all those years ago. In God's time he had gotten it right. He was the man for the job, just as his father had been. Like father, like son. He felt connected for the first time in his life. It was his heritage and he'd collect it. Eye contact, oh hell yes! He'd have that. He was excited. He had a plan if the cops came. If they didn't come, another day, soon.

.   .   .

"Oh, she's up," Dwayne said as they rounded the corner.

"Five of seven and outside scrubbing the steps. These old women, where do they get the strength? Tom said.

"Probably from God," Dwayne said.

"Probably," Tom agreed.

"Good morning, Mrs. Gonzales," Tom said.

"Who are you?"

"Remember me, Maria?" Dwayne asked.

"Oh, si si, come in, Thank you so much."

Dwayne followed the old woman up the stairs and shrugged his shoulders for Tom to follow.

"Sit down, it's good to see you."

"Thank you ma'am. This is my boss, Lieutenant Tom White. We have a couple more questions for you."

"About Hernan? I answered all those questions last night."

The police were here last night?" Tom asked.

"Si, and they took all Hernan's supplies."

"I'm sure they'll make sure they get to the right place," said Dwayne.

"They weren't nice like you," she smiled at Dwayne.

"I'll have a talk with them," Dwayne said.

"Mrs. Gonzales, may we look out your window?" Tom asked.

"He's not there."

"El Diablo?"

"Si, El Diablo."

"When he was out there, could you show us where he was."

"Si, you can smoke, I like the smell."

"How did you know?" Tom asked.

"You took your cigarettes out twice, then put them back."

"She's a lot sharper than we are this morning, Tom."

"Yes, she is," he said, as he lit a cigarette.

The old woman pulled back the curtains.

"He always sits there."

Tom looked out the window.

"Where, Mrs. Gonzales?"

"Right there, by the bridge, he drives one of those cabs."

Tom looked two blocks across the rubble of the old homes. There were three cabs waiting for fares at the Junction of the bus lines.

"You're sure he's not there now?"

"No, his cab is pretty. It shines, fancy tires."

"Thank you, Maria. Let's go, Dwayne."

They were in the car and moving.

"I'm sorry, Tom. I should have pumped her a little more. I feel terrible."

"Hey Dwayne, someone tells you the devil is outside, it's easy to brush them off as nuts. Forget it. I feel terrible, too. When we first arrived, we saw a shiny cab. We thought he was lost, or new."

"The killer drove right past us," Dwayne said.

"He hides in plain sight. That's what Dan said."

"Tom, I'm sick."

"So am I. Marco, and who else."

"Do we know what company he drives for?"

"Jim does. He went to talk to the cabby last night."

"What? Call Jim!" Dwayne said.

Tom picked up the phone. It rang ten times.

"Answer your phone, you bum. How the hell can you be a roofing contractor without an answering machine? He's always been a damn pain in the ass," Tom said anxiously.

"But you like him?" Dwayne asked.

"Yeah, he's nuts, but I do. Look Dwayne, I've got a feeling Willis will be at Joyce's getting donuts. Ready will be at the Lantern. Let's go over there and get them. We're slamming the door on this today. Come hell or high water."

"I'm ready, I want to see this animal."

"Never say your 'ready', it bothers me," said Tom.

"Ready, Oh, I get it," Dwayne laughed.

Tom was pumped. All he needed was one piece of information from Jim.

"Tom, was the name Ron P.?" said Dwayne.

"That's it. Good thinking, we don't need Jim. As soon as we get out of traffic and park, get the guys. I'll call the cab companies."

"Willis is over there, Tom."

"Good, go get him, don't get killed crossing the road. Ready's here, too."

Tom banged on the window and waved Ready outside.

"What's up? We're off, right?" said Ready.

"Wrong. Willis is coming over from Joyce's; you're with him. Sit tight. We've got the case in hand," said Tom.

"Got a suspect?"

"With a job and a first name."

"Great!" said Ready.

"Dwayne jumped in the car with Tom. He'll be here in a minute," he said.

Ready walked back to the car, after getting his coffee from inside.

"Tom, Alice said Sammy got hit by a truck last night. They just found him behind a store in Collingswood," said Dwayne.

"What a shame. How's she taking it?"

"Hard, real hard."

"Dwayne, I'm going in for a minute. Call the cab companies. There are only a few. Camden, Collingswood."

"Right, boss."

Alice ran to Tom as he entered the shop.

"Tom, I was going to take him in. But now . . ." She fell into tears.

"Is that it? Alice you treated him good every day for years, remember that."

"I know, but shit."

Tom held Alice. Dwayne had it; he was waving Tom out.

"Honey look, shut this place down and go home. I've got a case to close. It can't wait. I'll come by first chance I get."

"Sounds good. See you later. That poor little man." Alice walked away, openly crying.

"What company?" Tom asked.

"On Time Taxi," Dwayne said.

"Willis, you hear that?"

"Yeah, we're gone."

Both cars turned right and drove fast; it was only a mile away.

Tom parked out front. Willis didn't need to be told he had the back. Tom charged in the door with Dwayne.

"Hang that phone up," he shouted.

"This is business," the dispatcher said.

"Hang it up or you'll go to jail."

"Okay."

"You just got a call. You have a driver named Ron. I want to know if he's on duty now?"

"No, he's not."

"What shift?"

"Night shift."

Tom glanced at Dwayne. He knew this guy was it.

"His name and address, and don't call him," Tom said.

"I wouldn't warn that creep. Ron Philips, 20421 Rolling Hills Boulevard."

"Did he work last night?"

"Yeah, but something strange happened."

"What, fast, what?"

"He missed a fare, one fifteen at the Speed Line. He's always been on time. He never missed one before."

"He is AA isn't he?"

"Yeah."

"Let's go, Dwayne. Willis, let's talk a minute."

Willis and Ready hustled down the alley to the front of the building.

"We're going up slowly, this guy has nothing to lose. Ready, you and Willis find the back door. Shotguns, he makes a bad move, he's done."

"Dwayne will cover me at the front. Jim was supposed to talk to the suspect last night. I've got a bad feeling, he might know we're coming."

"You guys got vests?"

"I do." Willis said.

"No, Boss," Ready said.

"Stay back then, Ready. Don't take any chances."

"Tom, what about a warrant," Dwayne asked.

"What warrant, we're just going to ask questions. If the answers aren't right, we'll sit on him until we can get one. Let's move."

"Ah shucks, Tom," Dwayne groaned.

"Relax. After this case the D.A. will love you, the Captain can march you around and get elected. It's your collar."

"My collar!"

"That's right. This is my last case. I don't need it."

"I feel better now," Dwayne smiled.

"I thought you would, brown nose," Tom smiled.

Ron looked at himself in the mirror. He had a dream when he was a boy. A recurring dream. He had thought it was a man from Mars coming after him, but it was his own reflection. All those nights he'd been scared of himself. Full armor, head to toe. He laughed. He did look like something in a dream . . . no, a nightmare.

He'd heard the talk at the Cab Company. It would be today. Like father, like son. So be it, he was ready.

"20421, that's it," Dwayne said.

Tom nodded at the house. Willis nodded back and went to the end of the row homes and turned right out of view.

"Give them a minute," Tom said, mainly to himself.

"Dwayne, shotgun."

"For a few questions?"

"Dwayne, shotgun."

Tom's ears were red. Dwayne grabbed the gun. They watched the house. Steam was coming out an upstairs window.

"Maybe he's in the shower?" Dwayne said.

"Should be, just finished his shift."

"Maybe Jim didn't see him."

"Maybe, let's go," said Tom.

They got out of the car. A lady out front with two kids saw the shotgun. She walked over, took the baby out of a stroller and grabbed a toddler by the hand on the way to her home. They were inside now.

"Dwayne, stay back, watch the windows. I'll get the door," said Tom.

Tom knocked. He put his ear to the door.

"Water's running. He can't hear us. We'll wait a minute," said Tom.

Willis and Ready couldn't get the car up the alley. A few guys were pushing an old car. They parked on the street and walked the thirty yards.

"Willis, look out!"

"What?"

Ready pushed Willis down. Picked up the grenade to throw it; he didn't have the time. The explosion ripped him apart.

"What was that?" Dwayne yelled.

Tom smashed in the door. A shotgun was rigged to fire. Tom dove out of the way. The door was shattered.

"Hit?" Dwayne asked.

"Let's go," Tom replied.

Tom had his automatic; Dwayne was behind him with the shotgun. They saw smoke in the rear of the house. Tom inched his way through the house.

"Damn it, look at that."

"Kevlar Industries," Dwayne read one of the familiar looking boxes.

"Head shots, Dwayne."

"Right."

Tom went into the kitchen.

"Watch stairs."

Tom looked out the back door.

"Dwayne, call officers down."

"Right, Boss."

Tom could see Willis against a wall; he moved, he was alive. The smoke was thick but he thought he saw Ready standing.

"Ready report," Tom shouted from inside the open kitchen door.

"No can do!"

That wasn't Ready's voice. He was out there.

"Don't think he's gonna make it, but Ron's in a good mood. Wham, wham, wham! There, now he's out of pain."

Tom fired four shots at the man in the armor. He fired back with fully automatic pistols. He shredded the kitchen. Tom had hit the floor. He wasn't hit.

"Ron's going, now. Have a nice day."

He walked slowly toward the cab.

Tom fired five more shots. He knew he hit him.

"You'll have to do better than that," Ron laughed.

The cab burned rubber away.

"Willis, Willis."

"What, where's Ready?"

"Willis, you hit?"

"I think my legs are broken, I can hold on, get that asshole."

"Help's on the way."

Tom ran back through the house.

"Wham, wham!" shots out front.

Tom saw Dwayne slide out of the car. The son of a bitch was sitting right in front of the house.

Tom fired twice. No effect! The killer drove away; not fast, not scared, like he was going to church.

Tom ran to the car. Dwayne jumped in. They followed the killer.

"Can we stop him, Tom?" Dwayne asked.

"I don't know. Full body armor and we're outgunned."

"Follow him. Try to ram him if you get the chance."

The killer floored the taxi. They followed him. There was a work crew at the corner. The killer fired at least twenty shots. All four fell.

"What the fuck?" Dwayne said.

"Death walk," Tom answered.

The killer was off again. They followed. Tom fired at the car with the shotgun. He hit the rear tire.

"It's flat. What now, Asshole?" Tom yelled.

The killer drove on the flat.

Tom looked ahead. This time of the day, the Speed Line is packed. Oh no!

"He's going to the Speed Line. Ram him. We can't let him get on that train," Tom yelled.

"Tom, grenade," Dwayne slammed on the brakes. Tom ducked; Dwayne tried. The explosion took out the car.

"Dwayne, you hit?"

"Tom, my foot," Dwayne moaned.

Tom dragged Dwayne from the car.

Dwayne pushed the shotgun at him.

"Get him! Doris and Shelly were taking the Speed Line shopping."

"Too early."

"Go, they breakfast there."

"Oh, no!" Tom ran for the Speed Line. The killer had left his car in the street. He was walking across the parking lot. He fired shots at an office building.

"Look out," Tom yelled to a man driving right to the killer.

A salvo of shots rang out. The windows of the car were dust. Tom was fifty yards behind him. The shotgun was a good weapon but not at this distance against armor.

The killer turned to Tom. "You're always behind me, like at the hospital. The note."

Tom fired his pistol. He hit his helmet.

The killer fired at Tom as he dove behind a car.

"Love to hang around but I've got a train to catch."

Tom looked after the killer. He saw Dwayne's car in the lot. Why didn't the train take off? Automatic! It would leave on time. The girl's had been here. Were they on that train?

A squad car pulled into the lot. He didn't see the killer. He had no chance.

The killer's automatic fire tore through the car in seconds. It rested against a bus stop sign with the horn blaring.

The killer waved to Tom and went inside the station. More shots, not as loud. Ron was doing his filthy work, still.

Tom reached the door and opened it. Three girls in school uniforms were on the stairs. They were gone.

Tom raced up the steps and out onto the platform. Rifle fire raked the platform. Tom dove for the train. More shots. He was hit in the hip. He aimed the shotgun up the center aisle; a boy was in the aisle. Tom couldn't fire.

"Is he in your way officer? Can't have that."

Three shots rang out. People were screaming. A guy in a Teamsters jacket made a grab for Ron's pistol. Four more shots rang out.

"Brave lad, he really wanted the gun. But I've got two."

Tom could tell by his voice that he was enjoying this.

"Hey you, why the fucking nose ring? That make you a tough guy? Answer me!" Ron screamed.

"I'm not tough," he said.

"Damn right."

Two shots rang out.

"No officer, he wasn't tough," he laughed shrilly.

"What's your plan? Why don't you give it up," shouted Tom.

"This is my plan. Like father, like son."

"Who was your father?"

"Tony Philips, heard of him?"

"A sick piece of shit."

"I don't like that, and I've had enough of you. Throw out the gun or I'll kill these five people." Shots and screams sounded.

"I said throw out your gun."

"Fuck you, you're on a death walk. You're not going to spare anyone."

Tom jumped up and fired the shotgun. The blast hit him and knocked him off balance. Tom charged Ron. He fired three shots, hitting Tom in the shoulder and twice in the vest. As Tom was blacking out, he saw Shelly's face.

The killer was sitting in the aisle. Shelly and Doris were in the last seats. The killer was up now walking toward them. The train slowed down for the Ferry Avenue stop. A man rose up, across the aisle from Shelly and Doris.

"Not my baby!" Big Daddy roared as he charged the killer.

The killer leveled both pistols and fired but he wouldn't be stopped. Big Daddy smashed into the killer, sending him on his back. He fired wildly, hitting several people. One gun stopped firing; then the other.

Shelly jumped into the aisle.

"Don't load that gun."

"Wait a minute, Lady."

The killer rolled with his back to Shelly, desperately trying to load his weapon. Shelly ran to him, yanked his head back and shot him three times in the face.

She looked at Big Daddy. She heard Doris scream. She heard many screams. The train pulled into the station. Cops were everywhere.

Shelly dropped her gun. "He's there," she pointed at the man in the armor.

"Who got him?" a young cop said.

"Get the hell out of my way, go look after that woman, she's in shock," said Shelly.

"What?"

"Put your gun away, Goofy, and do your job."

"All right miss, I'll look after her," a sergeant said.

Shelly ran to Tom. People were moaning and crying.

"Tom! Tom!" Shelly screamed.

"Did I hear Big Daddy?"

"Yes Tom, you did."

"I thought so."

Tom blacked out. Shelly looked back through the train. She thought about her Grandmother. She'd had a bad trip on a train, too. Like her Grandmother, Shelly had survived.

.   .   .

"Tom, Tom, you awake?"

"What, who is it?"

"It's Dwayne, Tom. You're going to be okay."

"Why wouldn't I be, and why are you in my house?"

"Sergeant Cherry, he's still groggy and you're going to get me in trouble. We'll have to leave the room," the nurse said firmly.

"All right, I'm going."

"How is he, Dwayne?" Sugar asked.

"He's going to be okay. Without the vest . . ." Dwayne shook his head.

"You're not supposed to be up. Back to bed," the nurse said to Sugar.

"That's my partner."

"What can you do for him? Back to bed or no more snack bar. I mean it."

"Some mean nurses in here, Dwayne."

"Move it, I'm not having wounded cops bleeding all over my floors."

"Will ya get me a milkshake?" Sugar asked.

"All right. Now move!"

"Sergeant Cherry, limp over to your room now. He's going to be fine."

"Where's Willis Taylor?" Dwayne asked.

"He's in O.R. He'll be up soon. I want you all in your own rooms. It's two o'clock and other patients need rest, too."

"Can you get me a shake?"

"All right, move it. I've had it."

"I'm going. Thanks for helping us."

"You're welcome."

The nurse looked in on Tom. She took his pulse and read his chart. He'd be sore for a month, but he'd be okay. She walked back to the nurse's station and looked at her watch. Well, Shelly said to call as soon as he came up to the floor. Two fifteen a.m., but the nurse knew her party would be up. She picked up the phone. It rang once.

"How is he?" Shelly answered.

"Shelly, he's fine."

"Really?"

"Really."

"Thanks, Joanne."

"The shoulder wasn't broken, the hip isn't and he's got four broken ribs."

"Poor boy," Shelly said.

"He's groggy now, but by morning, he'll be okay to visit. How's your friend?"

"She's wounded as badly as Tom. Her father was wonderful and she loved him so much. She is sleeping now. It's just terrible."

"Dwayne will be released tomorrow. His ankle is broken and his foot was lacerated, but he'll be okay."

"It will be good for Doris to have him here. Take her mind off her father. He loved her so much."

"Shelly, I've got my rounds, I'm sorry."

"Thanks Joanne. I know you have your hands full. We'll get together."

Chapter Thirty-three

Tom was standing on Kings Highway, in Haddonfield, the center of town. He looked at the office. He thought it looked good. Shelly had done a nice job. The Historical Society had been a pain in the ass, but finally, things like color, material, had been worked out and it did fit the block and the town. It was only ten miles from Camden, but worlds away.

Shelly picked Haddonfield. Tom wanted to set up in Cherry Hill, but she had prevailed. Like Dan had advised, just go along, it will be the right way.

Cherry Hill really had no downtown. It was a conglomerate of housing developments. Shelly had told Tom, by putting the office in a town center, which Haddonfield had, they could cut advertising costs in half. She had spoken like Dan. Location, location, location! Tom smiled. Dan sure knew Shelly.

"Hey Honey, wake up and give me a hand," she called.

"More plants, Shelly?"

"I like plants. Take the big one. How's the shoulder feeling?"

"It's okay."

Tom held the plant and kept the door open with his foot. Shelly buzzed past him with a tray of fresh flowers. He could feel her excitement.

"Alice, take these please, I'll help Tom," said Shelly.

"In those vases on the shelf, Shelly?" Alice asked.

"Not all of them. I'm putting a few in the window."

"Where, Shelly?" Tom asked.

"Next to the coat rack."

"Alice. Everything okay?" Shelly said.

"I can't think of anything we've forgotten," said Alice.

"Good. Thanks, Sweetie. I couldn't have done it without you. Tom's just useless at this type of job."

"Well thank you very much," Tom said.

"Let's face it Tom, You're no decorator. But that's not why I married you," laughed Shelly.

"Since you put it like that . . ."

Tom grabbed Shelly and kissed her. She kissed him back.

"Teenagers, like damn teenagers," Alice said.

"Great, isn't it?" Tom said.

"Yeah, it is, guys," Alice smiled.

"Tom, Willis is here, Yahoo!" Shelly said.

Shelly ran to the door. Tom wished he could bottle her energy, he thought he'd make a fortune.

"How's it look, Willis?" Shelly asked.

"Dandy, just dandy."

"You want Tom to help you with it?"

"It only weighs about one fifty. I got it," Willis chuckled.

"You can handle it, but can the ladder handle you?" Tom cracked.

"Good question, Tom," Shelly said.

"Knock it off. I'm down to three fifty and it's been a struggle. I need a little support here."

"Don't listen to them, Willis. You look great," Alice said.

"Hold the ladder, Tom," Willis said.

Willis climbed the ladder, the eyehooks lined up perfectly.

"Move the ladder away, Tom," Shelly said with her eyes closed.

"I want to see it for the first time complete."

"Willis, will you please put the ladder in the truck?"

"You're the boss."

"Okay?" Shelly asked.

"Okay," they all yelled.

Shelly opened her eyes.

"Oh Tom, it looks great," Shelly said.

"Hey Tom, second fiddle, huh?" Willis chuckled.

"What can you do, Willis," Tom said.

"It's beautiful," Alice smiled.

"I like it," Tom said.

Willis read the sign, "King and White, Private Investigations."

"Let's cross the street for a look, Tom."

"Okay, Shelly."

She was happy. Tom had known Shelly wouldn't be about to sit around for long. It was her idea and it did have merit. Alice would have a better job, so would Willis. He had his pension, like Tom; with his work here, he'd be fine.

"Tom, it's beautiful."

"That's because you did it."

Willis and Alice walked into the offices.

"Shelly, I don't think Willis and Alice feel very comfortable here. They always stay inside, well most of the time."

"You surprised? A high-class white town. Willis and Alice are Camden born and bred. They'll get used to the snobs."

"Willis sure sticks out walking down the street, doesn't he," Tom laughed.

"How would he put it, Tom?" Shelly smiled.

"Oh, he'd say something like . . . 'I was in Haddonfield man, I looked like a baked bean in a bowl of rice'."

"Ha, ha, ha, yeah, that's it," Shelly was happy.

"Tom, we'll open in a month."

"That soon? I thought we were going to kick back for a while," Tom said.

"We are, Honey. A week in Miami with Dwayne and Doris. Three weeks with Dan in Tel Aviv. You'll be dying to go to it, you'll see."

"Give me two months, I'll be happier about it," said Tom.

"Oh Tom, now you're being silly. Let's go back."

Tom walked back across the street with Shelly. He thought he'd been correct. She'd keep him alive until he was a hundred or kill him in six months. Tom lit up a cigarette. Shelly opened the office door.

"Where are you going?" Shelly asked.

"Oh shit, I forgot."

"Well, don't. I won't have this office stinking of cigarettes, and throw the stub in the trash."

"It's a butt."

"In the trash," Shelly smiled and walked inside.

He'd be glad to visit Dan. He smoked. She was right. Maybe he'd quit, maybe not.

"Hey Tom, you allowed to go out?" Willis said.

"I'll have to ask, why?"

"We've been here all day. I ain't used to it yet."

"Uncomfortable?"

"Yeah, funny, isn't it?"

"No it isn't, but this isn't South Carolina, Willis. You'll get used to it."

"I'll tell Shelly we're taking a ride. We can pick up some lunch."

"Now you're talking," said Willis.

Alice walked outside with a bag of trash. She dropped it into the container beside the building.

"Sort of creepy, isn't it Willis?"

"Yeah, that's it, it's sort of creepy."

"Shelly says we'll get used to it."

"So does Tom. I guess we will."

Alice lit a cigarette.

"You going to miss the force?" Alice asked.

"I thought I would, but I think this job will be a perfect fit. The work will, anyway."

"I can't believe we'll be bored, not with Shelly kicking Tom in the ass."

"Yeah, it's great, ain't it?"

"Funny as hell." They broke up laughing.

"Tom walked outside.

"Let's go Willis, see you later, Alice," Tom waved.

"You two seem to be getting along," Tom said.

"We've got a lot in common," Willis said.

"Oh hell yes, she's a tiny white ex-con and you're a huge black ex-cop. It screams it," Tom laughed.

"We've got a lot in common."

"If you say so."

"I do."

.   .   .

Tom was dreaming Shelly was on the train. He thought he heard her calling him.

"Shelly," Tom screamed.

"Tom, wake up."

"What? Shelly, where's Shelly?"

"I'm right here, Tom."

"Shelly, we were up on deck. Everything all right?" Doris asked.

"Tom had a bad dream, didn't you fella."

"I guess I did."

"Were you dreaming about Shelly, Tom?"

Tom reached out and pulled Shelly into the bed. He kissed her deeply. "Yes I was, Doris."

"You hear that, Dwayne? You should wake up yelling for me. It's sweet."

"I do wake up yelling for you, Honey."

"You do?" Doris said.

"Yeah, but you're always asleep."

"Stop it Dwayne," Doris leaned over to Dwayne and gave him a kiss.

"Doris, what are those lights?" Tom asked.

"Shrimp boats, beautiful aren't they?"

"Yes, they are."

"We've got to go back to Miami tomorrow, but it's been a great week," Shelly said.

"This boat is great. Good name, too," Tom said.

"Yes, it is. *Big Daddy's Girl.*" Dwayne hugged Doris.

"So, are you going to be happy running the marina, Dwayne?" Shelly asked.

"I like it. Doris likes it, too."

"It's a good living. You'll be happy," Tom said.

"Daddy thought of everything, didn't he Dwayne?" Doris smiled.

"He sure did, Honey. He was the best."

"Let's drink to that gentleman. Doris, don't start crying. Remember, Daddy would want you to be happy," Shelly said.

"I'm not going to cry anymore. Shelly and I had a long talk about a nice lady. She explained a lot of things to me. I see things differently, now."

"Your Grandmother, Shelly?" Tom asked.

"Who else?" Shelly smiled.

"Her Grandmother knew a lot. A lot about the joy and the horror. We've had the horror, now the joy. Who's going to open this bottle?" Doris smiled.

"You know something, Dwayne?"

"What's that, Tom?"

"We've got two really nice ladies."

"I'll drink to that," Dwayne said.

"Shelly, what time's the flight?" Tom asked.

"Eight p.m. tomorrow. I can't wait."

"You excited, Tom?" Dwayne asked.

"Yes I am; haven't seen Dan in six months. I miss him."

"No trouble with the Palestinians, is there?" Doris asked.

"None Shelly couldn't handle."

"You guys did pretty well, yourself," Shelly said.

"Only someone with a great attitude would say that, Shelly. We were beaten," Tom said.

"You're never beaten as long as you have life."

"Your Grandmother?"

"Yup! And Doris, Daddy isn't beaten, you were his life and you still are."

"Now I'm going to cry," Doris said.

"Don't cry, Baby," Dwayne said.

"I'm okay, we're all okay. Poor Ready; no one ever liked him, but he saved Willis," Doris smiled.

"Can't figure that cracker," Dwayne said.

"Underneath all that bull, he liked people. I always knew it," Tom said.

"We've had a good week, the best of my life," said Shelly.

"Why the best, Shelly?" Doris asked.

"Because I'm pregnant!"

"Wow! I didn't think I could do it," Tom smiled.

Tom held Shelly on the deck. They watched the shooting stars over the Gulf.

"A penny for them, Tom."

"I was just thinking."

"Tom, we came out here to heal. You've got to talk about it, for it to pass. Doris has made more progress than you," Shelly said.

"But Doris didn't get a friend involved. A friend who didn't make it."

"Tom, everyone makes mistakes. Just say it."

"Say what?"

"Tell Jim what you want to tell him."

"Jim, I'm sorry."

"Feel better?"

"No." Tom's eyes teared.

"You will. What do you want to name your son?"

"A son?"

"Pretty sure."

"I always liked Lex."

The End